NO OUTLAW ON THE TEXAS PLAINS COULD OUTRIDE

THE EX-RANGERS

WILL CARSTON: A tough, hard-riding marshal, he was dedicated to the Texas Ranger creed—and aiming for well-deserved revenge . . .

CHANCE CARSTON: The oldest Carston son, he was an ex-Union soldier heartily sick of slaughter. But a vicious killing drove him to launch a private war . . .

WASH CARSTON: Will's wild youngest boy, his .44 was as hot as his desire for vengeance—and he was ready to set the Texas frontier ablaze . . .

T. J. FARO: A man of mystery, deception was his game—and he was playing the Carstons by his own deadly rules . . .

CAPTAIN MILES ALEN: The arrogant Yankee officer thought that taking command of Will's town would be easy—until he went head-to-head with three ex-Rangers . . .

1

THE
EX-RANGERS

RANGERS' REVENGE

JIM MILLER

POCKET BOOKS

New York   London   Toronto   Sydney   Tokyo

An *Original* Publication of POCKET BOOKS

POCKET BOOKS, a division of Simon & Schuster Inc.
1230 Avenue of the Americas, New York, NY 10020

ISBN: 978-1-5011-0945-4

First Pocket Books printing January 1990

10 9 8 7 6 5 4 3 2 1

POCKET and colophon are registered trademarks of
Simon & Schuster Inc.

Printed in the U.S.A.

This one's for
Don, Glenda, Jenny, and Harold
for making my life as a writer a pleasant one

CHAPTER
★ 1 ★

Some were saying the war was over. At least, that was the word from back east. Lee was supposed to have surrendered to Grant upward of two months ago, back in April. If you believed the rumor that had spread like wildfire concerning it, of course.

To hear others talk, on the other hand, it was far from over. Some ambitious Union officer had rallied his men down in the Brownsville area and attacked the nearby Confederate forces. That was a mistake, for it was old "Rip" Ford who commanded those Confederate forces. I'd known Rip before the war, when both of us were Texas Rangers. John S. Ford was his real name. Rip was a monicker he'd picked up early in life as a ranger. "Rest In Peace" is what it stood for, yes sir. Those overanxious Union boys found out how much death Rip and his boys could deal out that day. Reports had come in giving a total of thirty Union deaths and over a hundred prisoners of war amongst the Union forces. It was a clear victory for Rip and his boys, ragtag though they were. For at least a couple of weeks after that battle, they were still in the war.

But not a day ago word had also come down that Rip had disbanded his unit, he also being one of those who heard of Lee's surrender to Grant. I reckon he knew the war was over too. One thing was sure, disbanding your unit was a hell of a lot more preferable than surrendering them to some arrogant Yankee commander.

Whether or not any of this was true was up for debate. After all, this was Texas and we were so far west we almost got used to getting our information secondhand.

"Mister Will," Joshua said, bursting through the door to the marshal's office. He was tall and gangly, a mite past middle age but good with a Henry repeater when the occasion warranted. He also tended to act as though damn near everything he came across in life were new and exciting, which made him a good scout for me when he was out and about the small town of Twin Rifles. How the town got its name is a whole 'nother canyon. "They's a fight going on that . . . well, you ain't gonna believe who . . . I mean—"

"Why don't we take us a look, Joshua," I suggested, checking the rounds of my Remington .44 and replacing it loosely in the handmade holster I carried on my left hip in a cross draw fashion. I hadn't heard any shooting, but that didn't mean there wasn't going to be any, so I pulled the sawed-off shotgun from the rack against the wall and checked its loads as well before tucking it under my left arm. I thought a moment about putting on my brand-new hat, a piece made by a fellow named Stetson, but thought better of it. The hat had no form and made me aware of the odd stares I often got from wearing the thing. No, I'd leave it here.

I couldn't imagine who it would be that was fighting this early in the morning as Joshua led me toward the north edge of town and one of the two saloons in our little community. Most of the men in Twin Rifles were middle-aged like Joshua, men who had better things to do than go off to war. They were all good levelheaded men too, so all I could figure was that perhaps one of their sons had come back from the war and was raising hell.

Me, I was past middle age, pushing fifty from the north side, and marshaling this little community. My family was gone so there was no use working the ranch I'd once had outside of town. Being a Texas Ranger was the only thing I'd done other than the ranch, so I'd settled for upholding the law as a way of making my living after the war had started.

I heard a chair break as we closed in on the saloon.

"Now, Mister Will, you just remember what I said," Joshua warned. "You ain't gonna believe—"

"Let's find out what it is first before we start discussing the believability of it, all right?"

My deputy shrugged, adding a simple "Yes, sir." I noticed that when he stepped aside, he made sure to follow me into Ernest Johnson's saloon at a bit more distance than he would otherwise have done. I should have taken it for a warning, but ignored it instead.

I squinted when I pushed back the bat wing doors, but it wasn't adjusting my eyes to the light that brought my brows together. Joshua had been right; I didn't believe what I was seeing. The two yahoos battling it out with their fists didn't notice me enter the drinking establishment. Hell, the way they were going at one another's throats, it didn't seem like they would have cared either. Well, hoss, me being the law and they being who they were, I figured it was time they did take notice of who else was in the saloon they were slowly tearing apart.

Without a word, I handed the shotgun to Joshua and took up my makeshift walking stick as a weapon. I didn't swing that hard, mind you, but the bigger of the two felt it when I tapped him on the back of the head with my gnarled piece of oak. Trouble was it didn't faze him all that much. Sort of annoyed him more than anything. His madder-than-hell look turned to one of surprise when he saw who it was who had hit him. It was then that his opponent, only a mite smaller in height than he, took the opportunity to light into the bigger man with a left and right cross. Oh, it staggered the big one, all right, but not before he let go a quick hard right of his own that sent the smaller man sprawling across the sawdust and dirt floor. I reckon it was just crossing the big one's mind to come after me when I took hold of him by the stack and swivel and all but busted the bat wings of Johnson's saloon as I sent him flying out into the streets. He landed with a thud, raising a cloud of dust. I know because I followed him out the saloon entrance.

A fire had grown in me when I'd seen the two, just as Joshua must have known it would. I made a note to listen more closely to Joshua from now on. I approached the man I'd thrown out. Mind you, it wasn't because he was wearing a Yankee uniform that I was madder than hell at him. Shoot, boy, the man he was fighting was wearing a Confederate uniform—or what was left of it—and I didn't particularly care for the

4

likes of him either! No sir, uniforms had nothing to do with it, not for me. Not a-tall.

He was focusing his eyes on me as he glanced over his shoulder and got up on all fours, breathing hard. It was when he started to get up that I hit him with a hard right across the jaw, placing him right back on the ground. It dazed him good, just like the blows he had taken inside the saloon. But I was a mite bigger than the young man he was fighting who was eight years his junior, and I could guarantee I had a lot more fire than the two of them combined. I didn't give him much of a chance to even get up before I struck his jaw again, knocking him out.

When I turned to my rear, the youngster in Confederate garb was staggering out the bat wing doors, only half-conscious and bleary-eyed. His squint turned about as wide-eyed as mine had when I first saw the two, and I do believe he was about to say something. Me, I didn't want to hear it, whatever it was. So I hauled off and hit him just as hard as I had the other one. You could tell by the way his body fell on that boardwalk that he was nothing but deadweight.

"You kept your word, Will," Joshua said, slowly shaking his head in astonishment. "You surely did."

"Always keep my word, Joshua," I said, glancing at the two lifeless bodies. "Always."

A young woman ran out into the street and dropped to one knee beside the big man. Rachel Ferris wasn't more than twenty years old and pretty as a picture. But right now, she was about to go into shock. "My God, it's Chance!" she said, her eyes about to fall out of their sockets. "How did he—"

"Don't waste your lace doily dabbing blood off'n his face, young lady," I said in what must have seemed a snarl. "I put him there and he ain't worth it."

"Will Carston, you're a mean man," she said in a way I reckon was supposed to sound tough, just before the tears welled up in her eyes and began to flow down her cheeks. Women get that way, I reckon, especially over someone they're in love with. And Rachel Ferris was in love with Chance Carston, had been ever since she was sixteen and Chance had gone off to war.

"No, ma'am," I corrected, "vengeful, maybe, but mean . . . I doubt it."

"Pa?" the voice behind me said. I turned to see the young man in the Confederate uniform looking at me in a quizzical manner. That was the word the boy had been searching for when I knocked him out.

"That's right, Wash," I said, following it with, "although I ain't too sure it's something to brag on anymore."

"Ma ain't gonna like this," Chance said, rising to his feet. He was as tall as me and just as big in his build. In his thirty-two years, there had been times when he thought he was also as tough as me. Whenever I'd bested him, as I always had, he'd remind me how much his mother didn't like fights, particularly amongst family members. Cora always had been a peaceful woman.

"Your ma ain't got nothing to say 'bout this, one way or t'other," I growled. Then, in a voice loud enough for them both to hear—along with anyone else in town who didn't already know—I said, "You see, boys, your ma is *dead*. And if you two *children* hadn't gone off to war, she might be alive today."

I couldn't have kicked them lower in the belly than with the words that came out of my mouth then. The words had served to sober them both up. Perhaps they would also explain, in part, the hatred that had so filled my voice when speaking to them.

CHAPTER
★ 2 ★

I was you, Miss Rachel, I'd stay away from Chance till he got rid of his collection of fleas," I said. He was on his feet now and she was gazing into his eyes with the same moonstruck look of love I'd seen about her when my oldest boy went off to war. But love or no love, Rachel was still a civilized woman and the mention of fleas repulsed her as she took two steps back and gave Chance a thorough looking over, as though she could spot a flea on his body simply by looking.

"I could use a mite of cleaning up, Rachel," Chance said. By the look in his eye, I'd wager he hadn't forgotten how much it was this young filly thought of him while he was gone. Maybe he'd had her on his mind all that time he was gone too. Hell, I don't know. Such a thought did stir a goodly bit of pride in me though, I'll admit that. I reckon it was because I saw a lot of me in my oldest boy. Not the spitting image kind of thing some fathers look for and find. It was a mite different with me and Chance.

Oh, we had similarities all right. But we also had differences between us too. We both had blue eyes, but those of Chance were a cautious, cynical blue. I didn't have to look into them more than once to know that the war had done things to Chance I had no idea of thus far. I'd heard plenty of things about this war, but it had never reached this far southwest for me to get a firsthand knowledge of it. I reckon I'd be learning about the war the same as a lot of other parents whose boys had gone off to war and come back a good deal different than the day they had left. Yes sir, a good deal different.

"You go ask Miss Margaret won't she please make ready a couple of her washtubs and some hot water," I told Rachel. "You tell her she's got a couple of customers who'll chop up deadwood for it in return." I knew good and well Rachel would spread the news of my boys and their return as soon as she was within earshot of her mother, Margaret Ferris. "You boys tell Joshua which of these nags is yours and he'll take care of 'em for you. Then I'd sneak down the alley next to the Ferris House so's I didn't embarrass the woman and her guests."

Chance and G.W. were dirty, mind you, but you couldn't cake enough mud and dirt on those two to keep the red from creeping up their necks just then. They mumbled a few words of direction to Joshua and made a hasty exit from the street and the small crowd that had gathered during the whole fandango.

Ernie Johnson had a brace of pistols setting on the bar next to my shotgun when I went back inside to get what I thought were the hats my boys must have been wearing before the fighting commenced. A Union cavalry hat with tassels on the front must have been Chance's, while G.W. was sporting that Confederate gray hat and visor so many Johnny Rebs were seen to be wearing. Both were dusty as could be, either from a lot of trail time or lack of caring . . . or both.

"Never stops, does it?" Ernie said, setting a beer before me. I pulled out my pocket watch, saw that it was pushing eleven o'clock, and decided it was late enough for a beer.

"What's that, Ernie?"

He smiled, nodded toward the hats and guns next to me. "Still picking up after the boys, I see." I saw the humor in it and gave a short laugh my own self, remembering the number of times I'd complained to Ernie about that very thing while I nursed a beer and Cora did her once a month Saturday morning shopping. The thought brought back memories of the old days, and I found myself going back to the past as I nursed the beer before me.

It had been a good thirty some years ago that Abel Ferris and I had fought off enough Comanche to make it safe to build a town in this patch of loneliness. The only reason it looked worth staying for was the closeness of water. But we'd made a go of it and that was how Twin Rifles had gotten its odd but appropriate name. We'd held our own with a pair of Hawken rifles, fighting off anything and everything that got in our way and doing it all back-to-back. I reckon we were all young back then.

We'd each sent for our wives and soon started raising the Ferris and Carston families. At first it seemed so hopeless I didn't think we had a chance at

9

making a go of it, but Cora was the optimist in the family and kept reminding me that there was always a chance for things to get better. Our oldest boy was born that first year and it was Cora who insisted that we name him Chance. I remembered her holding the newborn youngster to her breasts that first day and smiling up at me. "Now you can't say that you've never had a Chance." It was her attempt at humor and I laughed. Mostly I was laughing that day because I couldn't believe I'd actually done as much as I had in that first year. That and I had a heritage to carry on my name. I'd always thought that to be important to a man, that he have a son to carry on his name.

Abel Ferris had died in his sleep one night two years into the war. Margaret had taken over running the Ferris House, the boarding house Abel had built over a decade before, when business had begun to pick up in town. I was only five years her senior, but she had proven that she could go from being a mother to being a successful business woman. It was something you didn't see all that often out here, and I had a good deal of respect for the woman.

I finished the beer and gathered my collection of guns and hats and cut a trail to the back of the Ferris House, only half a block away. Margaret Ferris was carrying a pail of hot water over to the curtains drawn across the bathing area. Rachel was gingerly taking the dirty clothes handed to her from behind the curtains, her face screwing up into the most god-awful look you'd ever seen.

"You'll never get these things clean," she said in disgust.

"Oh, I don't know," her mother said, examining the two pairs of shirts and pants. "It might take a couple of washings, but it can be done."

10

"Not those pants," I said, pointing out the torn pants legs of the Confederate uniform.

"True." Margaret sighed. I could see her mind was clicking as she spoke, knew it for sure when she turned to her daughter. "Rachel, go upstairs and get out an old pair of your father's pants. I'd say that Wash has grown to about that size by now."

Rachel turned a reddish shade of pink in the cheeks and made a quick exit.

"She says you were pretty rough on Chance and Wash," Margaret said, as though by way of conversation.

"Do tell."

"From the looks of them when they came stumbling in here, I'd say she was right." I had a notion Margaret was trying to get me to open up, but I wasn't ready for that right now. I hoped my silence was enough of a hint for her.

"Do tell."

"Some day I hope you say more than 'do tell,' Will Carston," she said in a huff and walked out of the room with as much energy as she seemed to have spent on her words.

I pulled back the curtain and let myself into the bathing room, placing the weapons next to the men I thought they belonged to. When they didn't complain, I figured I'd done the right thing. Chance's pistol was an 1860 New Model Army Colt's .44, while Wash had toted one of the more popular sidearms of the Confederacy, a Dancer Brothers model of the Colt's Navy revolver, also in .44 caliber. Next to Chance's tub of hot water lay a bowie knife. I must be getting old, for as big as those things are, I didn't recall seeing it on him before.

"If that Joshua fella ain't sold off my saddle, I've got

a Spencer that goes with this collection, as well," Chance said.

"Same thing goes for me, 'cept mine's a Colt's Revolving Rifle," Wash added.

My eyes bored right through the both of them, for they knew I'd raised them better than to be acting like loudmouths.

"I come back from the war, Pa," Chance said after a minute of silence that was getting deadlier with each additional second. "The war's over."

"No, Chance," Wash said, talking as though he were slowly realizing something that his big brother had missed. "I don't think the war's over. I don't think the war's over at all. At least, not as far as Pa is concerned."

"Learning insight with your age, boy," I said to Wash. "Catching on right quick, you are."

"Get it out in the open, Pa," Chance said in a hard voice. "I've had more than my fill of this war. I've got better things to do now that it's over." The mad was building back up in him again, but this time it was directed toward me. "You never wrote once. Not once the whole time. What is it you think I owe you now?"

He was asking for it, by God, and I was going to give it to him! I squatted, heard the bones in my right knee crack as I did, felt the pain go through me, and knew just as sure that I didn't care. Not until I got my say in, anyway.

"You had my address, sonny, so don't complain to me about not writing. If your mother had an address, I can assure you she would have written, even if I didn't. Near broke her heart that you boys didn't. Neither one of you." I tossed a hard glance at Wash to let him know that he was included in this too.

"What do you owe me? What do you owe me? I'll tell you pilgrims what you owe me," I said in as hard a way as I'd ever spoken to my sons. *"You owe me your mother's life, that's what!"* The words never touched anything but their ears, yet, they were acting as though I'd kicked them in their elsewheres. Their heads shot back as though they'd been spit in the face, and confused looks came over them. Slowly, without words, they looked at one another, then back at me.

"But—"

"My ass! If you hadn't gone off to fight that damn silly war, she'd be here now! If you hadn't gone off to fight that damn silly war . . ." My voice trailed off and all I could do now was see her that one last time. The sight caught at my gut and I couldn't speak because of it.

"And what," Chance said, but the bite was gone from his voice now. Instead, it was filled with a cautious curiosity, the kind I thought would match what I'd seen in his eyes.

"You'd have been there when they came," I said, my voice growing soft, but more from the hurt of it than anything else. "You'd have been there when the Comancheros came and raped her and killed her and burned the ranch to the ground."

"Jesus, Mary, and Joseph," Wash said in astonishment. Somehow I knew that the red creeping up into his face had nothing to do with the hotness of the water he sat in, nothing at all.

"When?" Chance was now speaking with urgency, as though he could do something to rectify the whole situation, to change the words I had just spoken.

13

"Three days ago." The pain was killing me, but I was a man and there were certain things a man did not do, and crying in public was one of them. Hell, crying was one of them. It was one of the hard things about being a man. You were allowed to grieve, but not to cry, and I hadn't. These last three days I had wanted to in the worst way, but I hadn't. "They made a strike just outside of town, on the south side, and I'd gone to help out. But when I came back, I found out it wasn't just the south side they had hit. If someone had only been there to help her out." I slammed a fist into the palm of my hand. It was useless, but it was all I could do.

"You got no right to blame me and Wash for what happened to Ma while we were gone to the war, Pa," Chance said, "no right at all, as far as I'm concerned." He paused only long enough to give a fleeting glance at his brother. "But you give me and Wash a chance to get a decent meal, clean our guns, and get dressed, and there ain't nobody in heaven or hell that'll keep the three of us from finding the sonsabitches who killed Ma. Nobody." He meant it. I knew that much for sure.

"I got a feeling another war's just begun," Wash said, and I do believe he was right.

I could remember these boys in their youth, when they would fight one another tooth and nail, then turn around and defend each other at the drop of a hat. Not an hour ago they had been at one another's throat over the color of a uniform. I'd declared war on the both of them and they hated that; I knew they did. Standing there, it crossed my mind that the only thing the three of us had in common at that moment was a last name and the same caliber ammunition for our weapons. But now they were feeling the same loss that I had felt for the past three days.

Things would change. If nothing else, the three of us would be back to acting like the three Texas Rangers we had been before this War Between the States had set us against one another.

Yes sir, things were going to change.

CHAPTER

★ 3 ★

One thing about Texas, we look out for our own.

No sooner was the war officially over than Lincoln went and got himself assassinated, leaving his Reconstruction ideas to the Congress to carry out. I knew it wouldn't be long before those carpetbagging Republicans from up North had Union troops sitting on our doorsteps, watching us like buzzards waiting to pick over dead meat. Going to punish anyone living in the Confederacy states for being bad boys and getting out of line, they were. Well, hoss, that didn't set well with me a-tall. Fact of the matter is, I had a surprise in store for those Yankee uniforms if and when they showed up.

But like I said, Texans take care of their own. I say that because our Governor Murrah and a handful of other governors from the southern states of Louisiana,

Missouri, and Arkansas held a conference in May to prepare us for the coming onslaught of Yankee soldiers. What they came up with were some rules for us Southerners that would make it a mite easier to get by these Union uniforms. What they made official, according to the order I got in the mail that day, was that *"officers and soldiers were to be allowed to return directly to their homes; that immunity was to be guaranteed against prosecution for offenses committed against the United States during the war; officers, soldiers, and citizens were to be allowed to retain their arms and to leave the country if they so desired; the existing state governments were to be recognized until conventions could be called 'to settle all questions between the states'; and after a certain date each state should be allowed full military authority within its own borders for the preservation of order."* It's a good thing they threw in that piece about us all being able to keep our own firearms, for I do believe that the Southerners in all the states would have taken up arms and fought another war over it, had they been told otherwise! At least we had our guns, and as long as I've been on this frontier, why, if there's anything I've learned it's that as long as you've got a good firearm, powder and ball for it, a knife, a pinch of salt, and a good horse, why, you can go anywhere and do anything!

It was afternoon of the same day the boys came back to town that I got that note from the governor's office. All of the command decisions I'd read in it had been approved over two weeks before. But like I say, getting the news about two weeks late was to be expected in these parts of the country. I'd left the boys to soak in those tubs for a couple of hours while Margaret did what she could to wash out their clothes. I'll admit that leaving the two of them alone in the same room like that might well have given them reason to take up where they left off, but I was willing to take the chance. Hell, I figured it would take a couple of hours of good soaking to uproot whatever it was that looked to be making a home in the dirt on those two boys. Besides, I had no idea where they had been, but knew that in due time they would tell me.

"Taken over Ab Layt's old office, huh?" Chance said, as he and his brother walked into the marshal's office I spent most of my time in these days. They must have made a visit to the livery, for each had not only his holster and belt slung over his shoulder, but a Spencer and a Colt's Revolving Rifle in their grasp.

"War does strange things to people, son," I said. I was talking as I slowly gave my two sons a going over with my eyes. Standing tall and straight as an arrow like they were, brought back a sense of pride in me. Or maybe it was remembering how Cora always put a firm belief in "cleanliness being next to Godliness." She was that way. "Ab's boy, Gerald, he went off to war, just like you two pilgrims," I continued. "Word come down that he was dead. Ab tossed the badge on the desk and lit out to find the truth." I shrugged noncommittally. "Can't blame him, I reckon."

"I take it he hasn't made it back yet," Wash said.

"Nope. Don't know whether he found Gerald or not. Might be he didn't have an awful lot to come back to either. Never can tell."

It was past the noon hour and neither complained of an empty stomach, so I invited them both to find a seat and clean out their rifles and pistols. The coffee was fresh and I had extra cups, so I thought we might spend a few hours together and get reacquainted in the afternoon. Maybe have an early supper and a couple of drinks afterward. But neither one of them was much on conversation, and after an hour of hearing nothing more than the metallic sound of the parts of a rifle or pistol being cleaned and reassembled, I said as much.

"After a while, small talk ain't worth it, Pa," Chance said. "Something I picked up along the way during the war. They'd rather you just keep your mouth shut so's you don't give away your position." He shrugged. "After a while you keep your thoughts to yourself and respond to orders only."

"Well, this ain't the war, son," was my response. After a pause, I added, "Lessen, of course, you figure me for the enemy." That raised an eyebrow from both of them, along with a weary but deadly look to go along with it. It was hard at first, but I smiled when I said, "I hope you boys didn't lose your sense of humor too." I didn't want the two of them going after me that day, for it had been me who had done the hitting of them that morning and my right fist was still a mite sore from that incident.

"Not all of it, Pa," Chance said evenly. "I reckon it's just been four years worth of grim experience for us. Tain't something you get over just by going home, you know."

He was right and I admitted it. I could remember reliving some of the battles I'd been in during the Mexican War, back in '46 and '47 after returning from the war. I reckon memory can be a beautiful thing and a horrendous thing as well, all depending on what your memories consist of at the time. Some of those battles we'd fought were enough to give a man nightmares for a lifetime. On the other hand, there were my memories of Cora and our life together that I could never forget either, and would never want to forget. Yes sir, memories sure were something.

19

"Young Rachel sure did take to you while you were gone, Chance," I said by way of conversation. "Don't recall a time I'd come into town that she wouldn't ask me ary I'd heard from you or not."

"Don't seem she's changed much on that account," he acknowledged. It was the softest I'd heard him speak thus far, and I could have sworn I saw a hint of red creeping up his neck when the words came out.

I didn't have any such announcement to make for Wash, who all of a sudden got quiet, a sullen look coming to his face. The boy had been that way a lot before going off to war and when he did leave I often found myself wondering if he hadn't gone just to be rid of the town. It was a mystery I had never been able to figure out. Chance set me straight.

"Them townfolk are after him again," he said, pouring more coffee for all of us. The look on Wash's face was now going from sullen to the deep, dark mad I'd seen in the saloon earlier in the day. There was danger ahead between these two, but that didn't stop Chance.

"I reckon rumors will kill a man, Pa," he said, all the time keeping his eyes on his brother. "What happened to Ab Layt's son is as good an example as any."

"True. But cut to the meat, boy. So far all you're doing is chewing the fat."

"Little Brother, here, he swore me to secrecy back then, but I reckon it's time it got out in the open. War 'pears to have done enough to his disposition." Wash was getting angry enough to drop his cup of coffee and charge head-on into his brother, much as I was sure he had done earlier. Chance, well, he'd throw his cup of coffee right into his brother's face; I knew that too. I reckon my youngest got the hint when I brought my makeshift cane down on his shoulder to hold him in place and tossed just as mean a look at him as he gave me.

"Go on." And Chance did.

George Washington Carston had been born twenty-four years ago, back in 1841. I named him after the famous father of our country because feeling ran high in both Texas and the nation about pride in our country. Nationalism I heard one newspaper fellow call it. Well, if that was the equivalent of the Spirit of '76 my granddaddy spoke about, then I reckon that's what we had. It was part of what got us into that war with Mexico; we were looking for a war and finally found one.

Just like that war with Mexico was a mite different than most we'd been through, G.W. was different from his brother. No less brains or gumption, you understand, no sir. Where Chance was the spitting image of me in some features, Wash was the direct opposite. He was a couple of inches shorter than me and his brother, with brown eyes and what you might call dirty blond hair. It was all a matter of heritage, and to hear Chance speak, heritage was the big issue. You see Cora was blue eyed too and had dark hair, nearly matching my own dark brown hair and blue eyes.

But people talk and it was the folks in town who were talking it up about how legitimate George Washington Carston really was. Apparently, it got to be a bother with Wash, what with hints here and there as to who he *really* was. When Chance found out about it, he threatened to do something about it, but Wash only wanted to be left alone. That explained some of the frequent fights my boys had gotten into when I'd send them into town for supplies. It also explained the coolness of the townsfolk toward them the year or so before they left to serve in the army during the war.

"Why wasn't I told about this?" I demanded. This time it was me who was ready to take on Ezekiel himself! I felt like a fool, not knowing my boy had been talked about like that behind my back. Yes sir, a damn fool. Hell, after all those tight spots we'd been in as Rangers, these two wouldn't confide in me on something like this!

"Wash didn't think it was worth bothering you about, although I can see now he was wrong," Chance admitted, gulping down the rest of his now lukewarm coffee.

"I got a notion the rest of the town figured you was gonna treat them like you did Chance and me this morning." Wash rubbed his jaw, winced at the tenderness he felt. "Can't say as I blame 'em either."

"I see." It didn't look like I was going to get any more out of these two at the moment, so I made a mental note to straighten out the people in this town good and proper one of these days.

There was more silence for a bit before Chance pulled out a piece of leather he appeared to be working with.

"Fashioning a holster, are you?" Wash asked, as curious as I was.

"That's a fact." When he said no more but caught us still gazing in his direction, Chance went into a mite more detail concerning what he was doing. "Cavalry holster ain't made for a civilian. Flap gets in the way. Holster will run any- and everywhere on your belt. Figure I'm gonna need something that's there when I want it. I gotta look where my gun is to get it out, why, I'm gonna be useless as tits on a boar hog."

"Sounds good so far," I said.

Chance nodded, winked at me. "Damn sure betcha. I get through, this Colt's gonna feel right at home at my side. Gonna cut a couple of slashes in the belt and fit her on it right snug."

Wash looked at me. "I knew that was why he carried that big pig sticker. Something handy like that."

"Damn sure betcha," Chance said, overlooking his brother's attempt at humor.

I glanced at my pocket watch. It was getting on in the afternoon and palavering or not, my stomach was telling me it was time to get fed.

"Joshua ought to be here any minute, boys. You set that aside and I'll buy you supper over to the café."

I thought I saw Wash wince when I said the words. The boy always did have a mite of mystery about him.

CHAPTER

★ 4 ★

The Porter Café wasn't but two blocks up the street. They served some of the better meals in town so I led the boys toward the eatery, hoping we'd get in before the supper trade began to trickle into the café. There were the usual nods of greeting from people I knew, but the glances they threw past me toward my boys were less than civil. I had the uneasy feeling that they plumb hated the Yankee uniform Chance wore and, as Chance had said, were "going after" my youngest son again, no matter what kind of uniform he wore. I don't mind telling you, hoss, the whole thing was beginning to stick in my craw.

Porter's had grown into a decent-size place over the years for a small town café. The café and the clientele had gotten bigger, as well as the menu. It wasn't until I saw the look on Wash's face as we entered that I took in something else that had grown.

"G.W.? Wash Carston? Is that you?" the young lady said, as though looking at a ghost from the past. She had red hair and the prettiest smile I'd seen in a long time. Big brown eyes that added to her beauty, and a freckle here and there, although I knew good and well she would be covered with them before the summer was over.

My youngest squinted hard, at first to get his eyes adjusted to the darkness inside, but then in disbelief. I do believe he was finding it as hard to imagine the person he was looking at as she did him.

"Sarah Ann? No, it can't be you," he exclaimed. "Why, you done . . . growed," he added in astonishment at the woman Sarah Ann had become.

"I'll say," Chance said, almost in a leer. "Right healthy, wouldn't you say, Pa?" The comment made Sarah Ann blush, even if it was the truth.

"That's a fact, boys," I said. "Why, she *sprouted* something fierce after you left, Wash."

"Mister Will, you shush," she said, her red getting deeper in color. "You're just embarrassing me."

"Simply telling the truth, my dear." And I had spoken the truth. Sarah Ann had indeed begun to turn into a woman after Wash had gone to war. She had been all of fifteen at the time, and I'll tell you, son, it wasn't just her brain that had grown, if you know what I mean. No sir. She had developed into one of the best looking young ladies in the town of Twin Rifles. No doubt about it.

Seeing the way the two reacted toward one another, I was glad I'd steered the boys in this direction, for I could recall Wash and Sarah Ann shying away from each other, the way you do when you're young like that. If you can remember those days, that is. I suppose that, like many a father, once I'd seen those two, I had it in mind that they must have been secretly in love, although you'd never know it the way they avoided each other. It was going to be interesting to see what they'd say and do after four or five years of not seeing each other.

"You're looking well, G.W.," Sarah Ann said, still standing there gawking at Wash as much as he was her. I reckon she was about the only other person I ever knew, aside from Cora, who ever had the inclination to call Wash by the name G.W. Don't ask me why, for I don't know and never had the desire to ask.

"You're looking right well too, ma'am," Chance said. He was still looking at the woman in her, at the healthy part of her, but he didn't do it long. Wash landed a well-placed elbow in his brother's ribs and Chance got the message.

"Son, let's get us a table," I said, feeling a mite embarrassed my own self, as I steered Chance away by the elbow. At least Wash would have a few minutes to get his thoughts together and visit with the girl. I don't mind telling you that by the time I took my seat, why, Sarah Ann was palavering like it was only yesterday since they'd seen each other, but Wash was still acting like he had tangle foot of the tongue.

"You're gonna have to stop baiting your brother, son," I said once Chance and I were seated. "You may think he's just your younger brother, but he's got enough fire in him to cut you off at the knees ary he takes a mind to do so. Mark my words."

"Not hardly, Pa. He's just my younger brother. Always will be." I reckon that's the trouble with being a younger brother. It's either an older brother who can be tough as nails, like Chance, or your daddy that you have to see if you can best at least once in your lifetime. But then, I never did know anyone who liked playing what those orchestra fellows called second fiddle. No sir.

Sarah Ann followed Wash over to our table, her eyes following him to his seat in a pleasing manner. When he sat down, I saw that Wash was still acting shy toward her. Whether they liked it or not, my boys had each found someone in town who could still appreciate them on their first day back from the war. As rough as I'd been treating them, I reckon that was some kind of consolation to them.

"Now, Miss Sarah Ann, here's what you have that cook get us," I said, hoping she could hear me through her stargazing at Wash. "You get us your best steaks, panfry 'em so's they ain't no red to 'em, serve up some of those biscuits you make so well, and throw in some fried potatoes. And keep the coffee a-coming."

"You bet, Mister Will," she replied, but she'd been looking at Wash the whole time.

"Woman cooks up a batch of biscuits near as good as your mother," I said, then realized what I'd said and fell silent. With each passing mention of their mother my boys had begun to be reminded of the fact that she wasn't there anymore. I reckon the grief process was a slow one to set in on the two of them. That or they'd been more places than I figured they had during their times away from home.

I reckon I had gotten so concerned about my own boys coming back from the war that I'd forgotten there were a whole passel of others doing the same thing. So seeing the Hadley brothers all but bust their way into the Porter Café kind of threw me for a minute. There were five of them, ranging in size from

27

big to little, all wearing the same Confederate garb Wash had been wearing when I first saw him. It would be a chore, mind you, but I felt confident I could handle that group. What threw me was the simple fact that they walked in as bold as brass. One of the rumors floating around had been that the brothers had perished in the war, and I said as much.

"Don't see how you could put any stock in that kind of rumor, Pa," Chance said. "Hell, they're too damned ugly to die." The Hadleys had grown up around Twin Rifles, but had never gotten along well with either of my boys. I recalled some of the bloody faces and black eyes my boys had come home with as a result of mixing it up with those characters. Seeing a frown come to Chance's face told me he remembered those days quite well too. But when they spotted us, it was Wash they set after.

"Would you look at that, now," the oldest one said. Carny, I think his name was. "The town bastard's back in town."

Wash would have lit out after him like a cat were it not for a firm hand I laid on his shoulder.

"Easy now, boy," I said in a calm voice. "You remember what I told you boys about having a big mouth never making a big man." Actually, it was harder than you might have thought, for it was all going back to Wash's heritage, and that I didn't like. To the older Hadley, I said, "I see you boys still got loud mouths."

"Would you look at that now," Wilson Hadley, the second biggest and second ugliest said with a leer. "Old man's still a farmer and sporting a cane to boot. Whatcha bet he's a cripple, boys?"

I pushed my chair back and got up, using the gnarled wood piece of oak. If I made it look like I was a mite worse off than I was, well, hoss, it was only to make these fools feel a mite more overconfident. My words, on the other hand, were real as could be.

"I taken an arrow from a Comanche who tried making trouble for me a couple years back, boy," I said, slowly making my way toward their table. I wasn't all too sure what the rest of the Hadley clan was going to do, but Wilson Hadley was going to eat his words before he got anywhere close to eating any food in this establishment. "Course, that don't really matter, does it?"

"Huh?" Wilson looked about as dumb as he was ugly. With that realization in mind, I made my move. As far as I knew, I was the only one who was on his feet at the moment, be it the Hadley boys or my own breed. Wilson was half-turned around on his chair, his lanky right arm draped over the back of the chair just far enough so's he could reach his pistol on his left hip with a mite of effort. Feeling comfortable is how he was looking. Being on the near side of the table made it easier too, so I grabbed a chunk of his lengthy dirty hair and yanked it back as I brought the blunt end of my oak wood up into the bottom of his chin.

"Don't matter, sonny, because on my worst day you could never take me!" I made sure to put just enough fire in my eyes as I had in my voice when those words came out. Applying a goodly amount of pressure to the bottom of his chin helped too, I reckon. "You best keep your mouth shut around me, boy," I hissed.

Then things began to happen. I half-expected that the rest of the Hadleys would have their pistols out by now and be getting ready to blow my head off with them, but the younger ones seemed a mite amazed at the way I was handling their older brother. I don't know if it was me being as old as I was or the fact that

I dared to walk into the five of them like I did. Or maybe they were taking in the lawman's badge that was stuck on my shirt. Whatever it was, they were real amazed about it, yes sir.

Like I said, things began happening. Carny was the oldest, but he was also the meanest of the lot. I don't know what possessed him to outright kick the legs out from under Sarah Ann when she came out of the kitchen with a couple of baskets of fresh, hot biscuits on her tray, but he did. Knocked Sarah Ann clean off balance, sending her to the floor and biscuits flying everywhere. That was when I heard two chairs behind me scrape the floor and knew that Chance and Wash had anted up in this game. I wasn't sure just how, but even now, after they'd been gone for as many years as they had, I knew they were still my sons and we were still Texas Rangers at heart.

"You start picking up them biscuits, Carny Hadley, or so help me I'll shoot you where you are," Chance said in a hard voice. When a confused look came about the elder Hadley, Chance added, "That was part of my supper you just spilled." He had that long-barreled Colt's out in front of him at arm's length as he walked toward Hadley.

"That's a fact, mister," big John Porter grumbled, as he came out of the kitchen. He was Sarah Ann's father, attested to by the huge shock of red hair and overgrown mustache he sported. In one hand he carried a butcher knife, in the other his Dragoon Colt's, which he claimed could kill into the next county. "I don't like to see food wasted." Carny Hadley paused only long enough to hear the cock of both Colt's before giving up the idea of making a fight over the biscuits. But throwing a mean glance at Sarah

Ann, who looked quite scared over the whole incident, well, that was the wrong thing to do.

Like some mountain cat up on the high ground, Wash came flying out of nowhere to land right on top of the older Hadley, sending the chair tumbling to the side. From the moment Wash was on him, he didn't have a chance. Carny Hadley was twice as big as Wash, mind you, but I don't believe he ever encountered anyone as fierce as Sarah Ann wildly swinging one fist after another at his face. Hadley was so stunned he could hardly manage enough energy to bring his hands up to defend himself.

"Back off of him, Wash," Chance said, "you're gonna kill him."

"That's the idea," his brother confirmed with a quick glance over his shoulder before going back to hitting the man.

"Wash!" I said, with as much authority as I'd ever used on the boy. It made him sit up and take notice. "Let him live to regret it. That's the worst medicine you can dish out to him now. Believe me." He didn't want to, I knew it from the look in those eyes, but he did. If not because I was his father, then because I was the law.

Big John belted his pistol and grabbed Carny by one arm as Chance did the other and the two men dragged the bigger one out of the eatery. I let go of Wilson Hadley's hair and gave him a shove toward the door as well, indicating that the remaining boys could leave as well. Wash was rubbing his bloody fists, although I wasn't sure whether the blood was his or Hadley's. He'd been hitting the man hard enough to break a few of his knuckles if he wasn't careful.

Sarah Ann began making a fuss over Wash as soon

as she saw that blood. Me, I figured I'd herd these bulls out of the Porter Café and get them headed out of town. It seemed like a chore that Chance and I ought to be able to take care of while Sarah Ann was taking care of Wash. I paraded out behind the Hadleys, who were leaving single file.

I reckon I'm getting old. When I got past the front entrance, I thought I saw Carny Hadley lying in the dust in front of the café, and the youngest Hadleys were walking out toward their horses. But where was Wilson Hadley?

"Pa!" I heard Chance yell, but it was too late. Wilson Hadley had stepped off to the side when he left and had other designs, most of them on me.

He hit me, or tried to hit me, about the same time I heard Chance yell and was trying to shove a fist into the cavity between my neck. Wilson had swung hard all right, but his blow had hit the upper part of my shoulder before glancing off the side of my face. But the blow was hard enough to knock me off balance, and I soon found myself falling to the boardwalk, losing hold of my cane. Then Wilson was on me and I felt a hard fist land in my stomach, winced at the pain.

I was waiting for more, but a red hand grasped Wilson by the back of the shoulder and abruptly yanked him off me. Wash had seen the attack and was now proving his energy hadn't waned at all. Wilson was damn near as big as Carny, but that didn't stop Wash from doing his best to discourage the man.

Carny was still lying there unconscious, but the other three Hadley boys had a sudden urge to show up their brothers in this fighting game. Two of them lit into Wash and soon had him pinned to the ground, while the third one made the foolish mistake of trying to take on Chance alone. In a matter of seconds he was

32

lying sprawled alongside his brother on the dirty street.

Chance grabbed each of the other Hadleys by the nape of the neck, pulled them off and back behind him while he flung a helping hand down to his own brother and got him on his feet. Then the two of them faced off the two younger Hadleys in what was a relatively fair fight, if not outnumbered. Mad will do that to you, son. Ain't nothing going to stop a man as long as he's right . . . and mad.

I know because I was going through the same thing with Wilson Hadley. "Cripple, huh?" I growled as I hit him hard with a left and a right combination punch. He staggered back into a horse and lost his balance, giving me a chance to work away at his midsection. If I didn't bruise a couple of his ribs, I damn sure did my knuckles for they hurt like hell. He was bleeding from the cheek and swelling up around the eye when he finally fell to the ground.

"Smart-alecky kid," I said, the way a father does when he's laid to rest any doubts some youngster might have about getting old taking away from your manhood. Not hardly!

Chance and Wash were standing there back-to-back, just daring any of the rest of those Hadleys to get up from their prone position on the street.

"There," I said to them, out of breath, "I knew you boys could get along." The words brought the two of them to looking at one another, first realizing, I think, that they had been fighting back-to-back, just like the old days. No words passed between them, you understand, but when Chance winked and his brother gave a brief smile back at him, well, hoss, that did wonders for my morale. But there was still something to be taken care of, still something stuck in my craw.

"Them steaks of yours are about as burned as they can get, boys," big John Porter said from the board-walk.

"That's fine, John," I said, still huffing and puffing, trying to catch my breath. "You set our table and we'll be right in."

A larger than usual crowd had gathered, but then, this was a larger than usual fight. Since they were about to disperse, I figured this was as close as I'd come to getting all of their attention at one time.

"Since I've got you all here, folks, I think there's something that needs straightening," I said, picking up my cane and rapping it against the side of the Porter Café to get their full attention. I do believe that Chance and Wash were as stunned as the rest.

"Boys," I said, looking down at my two sons, "you remember me telling you about how your mother was staying with her sister in St. Louis that year before I brought her out here?"

"Sure, Pa. Why?"

"Well, boys, ary your mother ever had a fault, it was not talking about her relatives."

"Get to the point, Will," someone shouted. "We all got supper to get back to, you know."

"The point," I mumbled, "yeah, the point. Well, the point is that your Aunt Lucille, why, she had the prettiest *brown* eyes and *blond* hair that you ever did see." There were still some confused looks out in the crowd.

"I found out today that some of you folks had a few doubts about whether G.W. here was an honest to God Carston. Well, folks, I'll tell you, G.W. didn't come from no one but Cora and me. That's the point. You start talk like this again and I'll take any and all of you on just like I done these Hadleys, and they're

34

'bout as tough as you get around these parts. Yes sir, folks, that's the point. Now, go back to your meals and gossiping."

They weren't any too pleased about that, but I reckon when you take away a part of the town gossip, well, it takes something out of the town gossip, if you know what I mean.

The Hadleys had heard it all and were saddling up to go elsewhere. Experience told me that they would want to take up the fight again, but not this time. Something had changed their minds and they were acting mighty peaceful all of a sudden.

On the way back into Porter's, I leaned over and whispered in Sarah Ann's ear. She turned red enough to give the impression of having been put afire, her mouth dropping open in surprise as I chuckled to myself.

True to his word, John Porter had set our plates out for us. They were filled with a steak each, along with side dishes of fried potatoes and a new plate of steaming biscuits. The coffee cups were filled to overflowing. I reckon both my boys and I had as yearning a look for that food as any you'd ever see, but we all knew it was one meal that would be eaten slowly at best. Not that it was a meal to be savored, although I'm sure it was. It was just that each one of us had done more than our fair share of fist fighting for the day, and like it or not that does tend to make you use your hands in a tender way. I know it did in my case.

"Now that's how you boys are supposed to be acting toward one another," I said with a wink and a nod as we all took our seats and spent a minute or so rubbing our knuckles before we attempted to pick up the silverware. From the resulting silence, I gathered that

Chance and Wash either didn't want to hear what I was saying or didn't care. I buttered a biscuit before I spoke again. "You boys got a bad memory, is that it?"

"No, sir," Wash said. He grabbed a handful of biscuits from the basket in front of me, as though to make sure he was getting his fair share of them. I noted that he'd lost some of his feistiness.

"It ain't a matter of memory," Chance said, a serious look about him as he grabbed the entire basket of biscuits from before me. If it was a gesture of madness he was wanting to show, he had accomplished it. "I'd just as soon forget all of it." The words brought on a frown from me that demanded an explanation, and he saw it. "Hell," he grumbled, "it's hard enough starting over. You saw how hard it was just now dealing with the past. I say forget it."

Chance turned his attention to the food before him, as though to say the conversation was closed. But he'd sure enough gotten my attention. Forget the past? He couldn't be that bitter, could he? I dug into my own food in silence, wondering if this was part of what the war had done to him.

"What did you say to Sarah Ann, Pa?" Wash asked, a few minutes into devouring his meal as best he could. "For not saying much, she sure does look like she stepped in it."

I chuckled, gently chewed the rest of my mouthful of beef before answering. "Noticed that, did you? Well, son, the pure and simple truth is that I told her she had better believe that you are and always have been one hundred proof Carston."

That perked my youngest right up, it did. A real sense of pride came out in that boy's face. Impressed, he was.

"Of course, I also told her that I wanted her to

36

remember that when it came time to give me grand-children," I added, doing my best to keep a straight face.

Chance near choked on the meat he was swallowing before he broke out in laughter. Wash looked like he was ready to near die on the spot. Turned the same shade of red Sarah Ann had, and he suddenly knew why too. Trouble was it looked like he was about ready to jump across the table at his brother as quick as he had Hadley. As many fandangos as had taken place that day, well, hoss, I wasn't ready to break up another one. No sir.

"I don't know what you're laughing at, Chance," I said, taking another bite of my supper. "I told Rachel the same thing this afternoon."

That shut the both of them up for the rest of the day.

CHAPTER
★ 5 ★

Chance and Wash had rooms at the boarding house, just like I did. I'd left the ranch and what little was left of it after finding Cora dead and the ranch burned to the ground. Margaret had offered the room at no charge if I'd supply her with firewood off and on, so I said yes. More than once she had made that sort of arrangement with someone who needed a room and had more of a strong back than he did spare cash in his pocket. It was nothing more than horse-trading on a smaller scale, but both parties got served well, so there was no harm done in the dealing.

When I woke up the next morning, I heard a steady swing of the ax out back and took to wondering if some beaver hadn't felled a tree and taken to building a dam for the river. It was when I threw some water in my eyes and took a gander out the back window down the hallway that I discovered it was no beaver at all. No sir, it was Chance and Wash hard at work breaking up deadwood.

"Damn fool kids," I muttered to myself as I watched them. As fast as they were working, I'd bet a dollar they had some kind of contest going to see who could do the most. They'd been like that their born natural lives, as far back as I could remember. Always competing with one another. Or fighting.

"I see you two are still hard at it," I said when I'd dressed and made my way out back with my razor and shaving equipment.

"You bet," Chance said with enthusiasm. I doubted that either one knew what I was talking about, so I let it ride and commenced to getting rid of the stubble that seemed to grow back more each day. Of course, I'd grown to easily identify the smell of Margaret's cooking. It was ham and eggs she was fixing, by the smell of it this morning. I had a notion that if you'd missed home cooked meals as much as my boys likely had during those war years, why, that smell alone might have been enough incentive to work as hard as they were at the moment. I reckon it doesn't matter how old you get, your sense of smell will do many things to your senses and the way you feel about things. Yes sir. The fixing of a home cooked meal is a good example.

"My, but you boys are really making quick work of my deadwood," Margaret said when she wandered out back a few minutes later.

"Don't pay 'em no never mind, Margaret," I said. "They're just showing off." The comment brought a disconcerting look from the pair of them. "Trying to work up a sweat so's they can get another portion of your ham and eggs is what they're trying to do." Each of the boys conjured up a look that could have been a death threat. I reckon they had gotten used to not being talked down to while they'd been away at war, no matter who it was doing the talking down, me included.

"Oh, Will, don't be so hard on the boys. I appreciate what they've done, I really do. Why don't you boys wash up? Rachel and I are almost done fixing the morning meal," Margaret said with a smile, and then she was gone.

"Wash don't look too awful bad," I said, "but, Chance, you make sure you take a razor to that chin of yours afore you come in. Looks like about three days of growth you've got there."

"Well, pardon me all to hell, *mister,*" Chance growled, rubbing a hand across his jaw as he spoke and looking a mite more mean than I'd expected, "but I already *did* shave." Stubborn boy. I never could figure where he got it from.

"Well, I'll be," I said with mild shock when the lad stepped close enough for me to inspect the work he claimed to have done. "Must be getting old in my old age," I mumbled, more to myself than anyone else. I took a step back and cocked a suspicious eye at the man I called my son. I'd have sworn he looked to have a growth of beard. I could just have sworn he did.

Chance smiled in a confident way. "Believe me, Pa, I've had more first sergeants rubbing a hand across this face than you could imagine. Near thought a couple of 'em wanted to get right fond of me . . . if you know what I mean. They couldn't believe I shaved regular either." He shrugged.

"I see." I coughed, spit, and mumbled something about us getting to the community table before the biscuits got cold. Having to discuss the mystery of sex never was my strong suit.

I took to cleaning up my shaving materials while the boys waited on me, but all of a sudden I became all too aware of them being there. You know what I mean. It's the kind of sensation you get when someone's staring straight into your back, and you know good and damn well they're doing it. It's an odd feeling but a telling one just the same. Sure enough, when I turned around there they were, staring at me like the day was half through and all business about it.

"I see." Indeed I had seen that stare before. I'd seen it on their faces years and years ago when, as youngsters, they had behaved better than they should and wanted one more piece of hard rock candy for their efforts. It also crossed my mind that maybe I was falling into the same trap a woman does and constantly seeing my boys in the past instead of as they were in the present. "Well, what is it this time?"

"Chance and me are wanting to know," Wash said, sticking with the all-business approach.

"Know? Know what?" I scowled at them. I'll confess that youngsters or grown men, I never would take kindly to being talked down to by my own boys.

"We want to know what you're gonna do about Ma," Chance said. He had a deep, grumbling voice when he first got up that could only be cured by a couple of cups of coffee. I remembered that now, hearing him talk. "Ain't been back even twenty-four hours and all you've said is she's dead. People around this town don't want to do much talking about it either."

"That's likely 'cause what happened to her is none of their business, son." My voice had softened considerably, more from bringing up the horrid memory than anything else.

"Well, damn it, it's our business," Wash blurted out, "for she was our mother."

Under any other circumstances, I would have knocked him flat on his keister, but Cora was the subject and it would be some time before I'd get over the loss of her or the memory of how much energy the woman exuded by her very being. Now she was gone and so was everything she had been to me; I was reminded of this most strongly when the subject of her came up.

"That's what they taught you in the army, is it?" I said in disappointment rather than the rage I should have felt at Wash's insubordination. "Cuss a man ary you disagree with him, even if it's your own father?" I shook my head. "That's sad, boy."

"Will," Margaret said from inside the door. "The food's getting cold."

As though to ignore them, I headed toward the door and the food my stomach told me it was time to eat.

"Pa," Chance growled in a voice that was intentionally low. "I gotta know." It was a demand, not a request.

Over my shoulder I scowled at him. "You'll know, sonny. Before the day's out you'll know. Guaranteed." It was all either one of us needed to say about the subject for the moment.

Chance and Wash were probably right about having a right to know about their mother sooner than I had let on, but damn it, it was hard talking to them, hard to even welcome them home when I felt the way about them that I did. Nothing was easy anymore.

Pretty as Margaret and Rachel were, you would have had a hard time getting any conversation out of the three of us once we sat down before the steaming hot plates of scrambled eggs, coupled with two thick slices of ham to go along with them. Add to that attraction a nearby stack of hot biscuits and a handful of other strangers at the table, and eating wasn't a pleasure or a necessity; by God, it was a contest at Margaret's table! Rachel did her best to keep the coffee cups filled, but it was purely a chore, yes sir. Not a word was said by those at the community table until the plates were empty and we took to letting the meal settle over the rest of our coffee.

"Margaret, you set a fine table, as always," I said. It had become a daily compliment to her.

"Why, thank you, Will," she said with a smile.

"You set a fine table, Miss Margaret," Chance said, surprising us all by using the napkin to wipe his mouth off.

"Best food I've ate in I don't know how long, ladies," Wash said. "I thank both of you. You need any more wood chopped, you just let me know."

"Won't argue with any of these gents, ladies," a voice foreign to me said. I'd been a lawman long enough so that I got nosy just out of force of habit, although I suspicioned I had a mite more tact than either of my boys would have shown.

Fact of the matter was, I was so taken by the boys being back and the early morning prospect of having my morning meal with Margaret—something I had learned not to take for granted—that I had clean overlooked the rest of the people setting at the table. I gave them a quick looking over and saw the usual handful of those passing through. But the one who had spoken up was wearing a Union uniform with captain's bars on his shoulders. I reckon the only reason he didn't get the same god-awful look that

43

Chance had gotten the day before was the fact that the rest of his companions at this table, other than me and my boys, couldn't have cared less. Still, he immediately bothered me. Not the uniform, you understand, but the man.

"By the way, ma'am," he said, standing up to his full height as he readied to leave, "I'll be wanting to know if you could put me and some of my men up in a couple of days or so."

"Certainly, sir," Margaret said, ever the pleasant person. "Shall I assume you'll be paying in cash?"

"I'll make sure that you are, ma'am," he said, nodded, and doffed his cavalry hat before leaving.

"You be careful of him, Margaret," I said, finishing my cup of coffee and readying to leave my own self.

"Why? He seems harmless enough."

"Margaret, I heard 'bout a fella named Quantrill not long ago, who is supposed to have the looks of a school teacher," I said, strapping on my six-gun.

"And?" Apparently, Margaret hadn't heard the story about Quantrill that I had. Me, I didn't have the time to tell her about it.

"It's a good thing you didn't live in Lawrence, Kansas a couple of years back, Margaret. A good thing."

Margaret had a confused look about her when I left. Chance and Wash, well, I don't know if they were either not up to arguing that early after a meal, or if they knew better than to interrupt me when I was speaking. Either way they remained silent as I walked out of the boarding house and they followed.

"Damn hat," I said under my breath, as I entered the marshal's office and removed my cover.

"What's wrong?" Chance asked.

"Newfangled headgear some fellow named Stetson

44

is putting out," I said. "Good enough to carry a gallon or two of water for a thirsty horse, mind you, but I don't know about a man wearing it. No sir."

"What's wrong with it, Pa?" Wash said. "I seen all sorts of concoctions they called hats in places I've been."

"I don't know," I said in a grumble. "Makes me feel like I've got a peaked head."

"Shouldn't bother you none," Chance said with that grin of his, "you've got enough snow around the sides."

I cocked a malicious eye toward Chance, the both of us knowing he was as full grown as I was, and had been for some time now. Still, I was the father and he was my son, always would be. "You know, young man, you still ain't too old to send out to find the switch you want to get beat with." After what we'd been through the day before as a family, I reckon there wasn't any question as to who was the boss in this clan. It only took a moment or two of silence for it to sink into Chance's mind. Or maybe it was the bruises that were still hurting that brought back the memory that I would follow up what I said I would do, just as I always had.

"You know, Pa, one of the things I learned during the war was how to be versatile," Chance said. It must have been a new word for him, for he pronounced the last part *tile.*

He then proceeded to bring the flat of the side of his hand down across the middle of the top of the hat, as though cutting it from front to rear with a knife. He just did it gentler than if it had been an actual knife he was using. Then, using both hands now, he pushed the crease down in the center with the fingers, slowly working the hands away from each other as he got

45

further down. By the time he was through, which wasn't but another minute or so, he had cut the rounded top down a few inches and flattened out the top of the hat so it had the feature of being flat and cutoff. To add the final touch, he held the top side of the hat within his huge fingers and punched the inside of the Stetson with the other fist, pushing the inside back toward the top so it was even with the rim, forming a small sort of ditch between the top of the hat and the edge of the smaller stove top I now had to contend with.

"Do what you like with the brim of the hat," Chance said, handing me the hat. "At least your head won't feel so peaked now." He winked at his brother, although I suspicion he figured I was too taken with the newly formed hat to notice. But I did. It's part of my job, remember?

"Well done, Chance," I said, examining his creation. "I would add that my hat's off to you, but I'd likely get some smart ass remark, so I'll pass on that."

The grin he gave me was enough satisfaction for the boy, I think. Talked his way out of getting a switch taken to his hide again, he had.

I was trying the hat on and looking at myself in the mirror, gauging how I now looked, when the door opened and in came the young captain in his Union attire.

"You're the law around here, are you?" he asked in a rather crisp voice that had an air of authority about it now. When I nodded silently, he added, "If I'd known that back at the boarding house, I'd have talked to you about this matter back there."

"Long as you get the words out, I reckon it don't matter where you say 'em," I said. "By the way, Captain, you got you a name to go with that rank?"

"Alen. Captain Miles Alen."

"Nice to meet you," I said, sticking out a paw, although in the back of my mind I confess to having my doubts. The man still had a distrustful look about him. Or maybe it was simply that I'd had my fill of people throwing their rank around ever since the war had started. Hell, if any of them would have stopped to think about it, why, it didn't make a damn whether you were a private or a general. In the end you bleed and you breath, and taking away the use of both of those functions to the body usually results in death, no matter what kind of stripes or silly little insignia you're wearing. Fact of the matter was, I'd made a resolution to start throwing a mite of my own weight around the next time someone tried that kind of stuff with me. And it was looking like Captain Alen was going to be the one to get the first dose of me.

"I've come to take over the town," the young captain said. Oh, he still had that air of authority about him. It's just that when he uttered those words about taking over the town, well, he said them like he was a man who had come to stay, the intonation being that you'd better get used to it or leave fast.

"Do tell," I said, calm as could be. "You feel like explaining why, Captain? Just a matter of curiosity, you understand."

He said nothing, instead handing me a sheaf of papers he suddenly produced from the inside of his shirt blouse. The look on his face only got harder as he watched me leaf through his orders. I think it bothered him that I didn't shrivel up and crawl back in some corner, particularly at the sight of his uniform and his presence.

"Well, son, those are real nice sentiments," I said, when I handed the papers back to him. "They really

47

are." What his papers said was that there was going to be a military occupation of the southern states that were a part of the Confederacy during the war until it could be determined that their governments had been reconstructed to meet the criteria of the most precious Union of these United States.

"I get the impression you don't like what those orders say," Captain Alen said in a way that made me wonder if he wasn't taking a real joy in the delivery of such news. It was almost as though he took a certain amount of pride in looking down his nose at people like us. The trouble was that all too often men like Alen, who enjoyed looking down their nose, wound up riling up people who responded by looking down the end of a gun barrel in return. Some people never learn.

"That's a fact, sonny." I was feeling a mite uppity my own self all of a sudden, and like I say, I'd had my fill of people like this captain.

"The thing is, Captain Alen, ain't nobody in this town ever fought in your War Between the States or whatever you heroes are calling it now. Oh, we've all got plenty of sons who went off to war, and some of them are even beginning to trickle back in, like these two." I threw a thumb over my shoulder at my sons. Chance was back to working on his handmade holster and paying no never mind about what was taking place now. At least, that was the way it looked. Wash was sipping some coffee and toying with that Dance Brothers six-gun of his. Here again, things weren't what they seemed, for I had a solid notion that if this captain made one wrong move, why, my youngest son would have killed the Yankee uniform on the spot, and if there happened to be a Yankee soldier filling the uniform, why, that was too bad. These boys of mine had only been back for a day, but I was catching on real fast to the changes war had made in them. Yes sir.

These weren't the same young men who had ridden with me as rangers before the war. The war had aged them somehow, changed them in a way that I wasn't sure I knew or liked. Mind you, they were still family, but the longer they were back the more I found myself wondering if it should have been this hard to get used to them. Yes sir, the war had changed them. Now all I had to do was figure out how.

"Fact of the matter is, your war never even got this far south, or west, whichever direction you're coming from. Only thing we got was bad news about our boys dying here and there in battle sites and towns we never heard of and cared less about. So you see, Captain, all we've got a yearning to do now is get our boys back, if they come back, and get on with life, as small as it is in these parts.

"It really is nice to see a piece of paper like you've got that says we need to be baby-sat like some long-lost soul coming in from the desert. I'm sure that whoever wrote that had genuine concern in his heart for what he had in mind. Yes sir. But this here town is as grown up as I am."

"And what the hell is that supposed to mean?" Alen said, getting a wee impatient.

"It means he founded and built this town about five years before you were a glimmer in your daddy's eye," Chance growled. He had shifted in his seat, still working on his holster. The difference was that his Colt's Army Model was now in the holster and the business end of the six-gun was pointing directly at our young captain's belly.

"Don't let him fool you none, Captain," Wash said, still playing with his Dance Brothers weapon. "Next to talking to Miss Margaret this morning, this is 'bout as civil as he's been since yesterday morning. Beat the living bejesus out of us, is how he said welcome back. That's a fact."

"He's right," Chance said. "And me and Wash can take care of ourselves. I figure if you're somewhere between Wash's age and mine, why, Pa'll have your hide nailed to the back of that door in thirty seconds . . . or less."

"My orders still stand," was all the Union officer could think to say.

"That's fine, Captain," I said. "Far be it from me to stand in the way of military orders. You want to occupy this town, why, you go right ahead. Yes, sir." I gave him a brief smile before looking at him in as serious a manner as I could muster. "Just don't try to run the town." The words shocked him, maybe because I was the age I was and he was the age he was and held the rank he did. He definitely wasn't used to being bucked by a lowly civilian. "Honest, Captain," I said in a soft but firm voice, "people in this town won't let you. Guaranteed."

He either didn't know what to say to that, or figured there wasn't anything left to say, for he wheeled toward the door and left in an abrupt manner. I wondered if he'd ever been on the losing side of a battle during the war. If he had, he hadn't learned to take defeat gracefully. But then, I reckon few people ever do, no matter what they carry as a rank or position.

"Wash, you'd better pour us all a cup of that black stuff," I said, when the captain was gone. "When Joshua gets back from his meal we got some riding to do."

CHAPTER

★ 6 ★

At first all I got was a blank look from the two, the same type of look I'd gotten from them years ago when I pulled a surprise on them and they were just a couple of kids. Hell, compared to me they were *still* a couple of kids! So was the captain, for that matter.

"You'll see," was all I said, leaving their minds to wonder.

When Joshua returned from breakfast, I instructed him to take charge of the place, as he usually did with little problem whenever I was gone. He assured me the town and the marshal's office would still be there when we returned. He needn't have, for I had as much faith in my one and only deputy as I felt I would ever need to have. It was just that Joshua always wanted to make sure you knew he was doing his damnedest whenever you wanted him to do something. I reckon some people are like that.

Nathan Potts, who ran the town livery stable, had done a fine job of fixing up my boys' horses. In the twenty-four hours since they arrived in town, Nathan had fed and curried the animals so they not only looked decent again, but likely felt like it as well. Cora had always tried to impress that upon the boys, some little saying she had about cleanliness. But the boys had grown up to take on the belief of most men who go out into the world these days, that belief being that cleanliness is next to impossible. Anyway, I made a mental note that both my boys and their mounts were looking considerably better than the first time I'd seen them yesterday.

"Good to see you two back," Nathan said as we entered the livery. But his words only gave pause to my boys and they stopped and looked at Nathan before shaking their heads. Nathan, by the way, is as black as the ace of spades, and damn near as old as me, if not older. The both of us had the good sense not to make aging a topic of our conversations, knowing that life can be depressing enough as it is without the constant reminders of how long a body's been living it. But I couldn't help wondering if Chance and Wash weren't silently asking themselves if the man before them wasn't what the fighting they had been doing had been all about. I let the silence ride for a minute or so before I saw a look of concern cloud up Nathan's face.

"Don't pay no never mind to 'em, Nathan," I said, half smiling. "They ain't seen you in some years now. Been gawking at everything and everybody since they come back, they have. Getting used to their hometown all over again, can you believe it?"

"If you say so," was the liveryman's reply, but his eyes said different. For the first time since my boys had come back, I found myself wondering what it would be like once they got settled in again. Or was there too much that had changed, had they changed too much, to ever settle back in to a place like Twin Rifles. I had a mission I was taking these two youngsters on, but I was getting curious about other things too.

"You boys work with coloreds?" I asked once we were heading out of town. "I mean did they have 'em in your units?"

"Nope. Never saw a one," Chance said.

Wash shrugged. "Same here. I don't know 'bout Chance, but once I left here, when the war started, I never did see a black."

"He's right," Chance said. "You go off to fighting for something, I reckon you get curious about what it is you been laying your life on the line for." The more he spoke the more he became embarrassed about what he was saying.

"And you two find it hard to believe that you could have been fighting for the likes of Nathan Potts," I said, completing what I figured to be their line of thought.

"Well . . . yeah, I reckon so, Pa," Wash said. Even under the well-tanned face, I could see the boy flush some.

I reined in my mount, took a gander at each of my boys, one on either side of me. The town was barely in sight, but I had something I thought needed saying and this was as good a time as any.

"Let me tell you something, boys," I started. "Mind you, I've got no time for starting fights, for we've got things to do today. But you might's well know it from the start. Far as I'm concerned, that so-called war you youngsters fought was pure politics. Ain't a war I seen fought that wasn't politics. Hell, I was in the Mexican War and that wasn't nothing but politics, sure as shooting. You gotta know that, because that's how I feel about the whole mess.

"The second thing you've got to know is that even if that war was about fighting for freedom for the coloreds, ain't neither one of you got no reason to look on Nathan Potts as what you think your average black man is supposed to look like."

"I don't understand what you mean," Chance said, frowning.

"You study old Nathan next time he signs his name," I said. "You'll see." There were things these boys were going to have to find out for themselves, and by God, I wasn't about to make life any the easier for them in the finding.

I dug my heels into my mount, spurring the horse ahead as the two lads stayed behind for the better part of our ride, talking back and forth amongst themselves.

There was a lot these boys would have to get used to, a lot that had changed since they'd left home. I reckon it was just as well that they be lost in their thoughts as we rode out of town, for it gave me time to gather mine, and I don't mind telling you that they were painful ones.

The boys had simply followed me as we left town, not asking any questions because they knew full well I'd speak when I was ready to. I guided them north by west out of town. All the while we rode I could hear them behind me, talking away like the town gossips just coming from a convention meeting of one sort or another. Likely it was good that they didn't ride beside me, for the muscles began to tense more and more as we rode further and further in that direction. The rage increasingly began to fill me as we rode.

"Damn!" I muttered when we rode into sight of what was once a ranch house, once our home.

"Jesus, Mary, and Joseph!" Chance said in as soft a breath as I'd ever heard him speak in.

"Well, I'll be damned," Wash said in the same astonished tone.

"You ought to be," I said in a voice that had suddenly turned harsh. "Ary both of you had been here . . . hell, if *either* of you had been here." I paused a moment, remembering it all, the sight of the black smoke as it curled toward the sky, the terrifying scream coming from a voice that could only belong to my Cora. I remembered feeling my heart sink deeper the closer I got to what had once been a house on fire. "If either one of you had been here, what's left of your mother wouldn't be buried over there!" I all but shouted in a rage I hadn't yet learned to control.. For the first time in a long time I saw genuine fear in the two men sitting in their saddles as my arm shot out in a direction that led to a grave site and a crude cross that marked the grave of Cora Carston. The thought of it had made me want to cry more times than I could remember, more times than I wanted to count. Instead, all that welled up in me was an unbridled rage at both of my boys who *should* have been there to protect their mother while I was gone, and the sorry bastards who had done this deed.

I don't think I could have kicked these two any harder in the gut than I did with those words I had just spoken. In silence and on the verge of tears themselves, Chance and Wash dismounted, dropped the reins of their horses, and removed the hats from their heads as they walked over to the grave of their mother. After staring at the grave and its marker in silence, the two walked around the area and looked over what used to be a house they knew well.

"Looks like the work of Quantrill," Chance said, taking in the burned remains of the ranch house.

"Not hardly," Wash said in defiance. "More like those Red Legs of Jim Lane's." He spat the words at his brother and the fight was on.

Chance hit him low, doubling up his brother like a piece of paper being folded over. Then he brought a huge hard hand down on top of Wash's neck and the boy crumpled to the ground in pain.

"That'll teach you," Chance growled, looking down at his brother triumphantly. By then I had slid out of the saddle and was approaching the situation.

"Son," I said softly. Then, when he looked up, I hit him with a surprise right that he wasn't expecting any more than Wash had been expecting Chance's blows. It staggered him, sending him reeling backward but not recovering soon enough. I stepped across Wash and let go a hard left that near cracked my knuckles when it landed alongside Chance's jaw and sent him to the ground like so much timber being felled up in the northwest.

"Is that all you can think about?" I asked, standing between the two of them as they slowly got up. "Fighting with one another over that goddamn war, that goddamn uniform?" In case they hadn't guessed, I was mad and I let them know it. "It was *stupid,* damn it, the whole damned war was *stupid,* do you hear me?" I was all but yelling now for I wanted them to hear what I thought, didn't care what they thought, only wanted them to know how outraged I was with them for letting their mother die like she did.

Wash was still reeling some from being hit below the belly, but Chance had a look about him that said he was willing to carry this fight on until sunset if need be. Me, I could have stood there and fought him toe-to-toe day in and day out for a month, I was that mad.

"You goddamn birds have got a lot of guts showing your faces back here! Damn fools, the both of you." I hadn't lit into them like this in years, which is likely why they got to looking angry instead of fearful. But they listened.

I started with Wash. "I can understand you being adventuresome, boy, and I wouldn't mind you riding with Ben McCulloch. No sir. Good man, he was. Good ranger too. But you didn't have the guts to even confront me about it! You just sneak off into the night to ride with McCulloch and his bunch. Knew he was riding for the Confederacy, didn't you?"

"Yes, sir," he replied, as though he'd gotten used to being chewed out by high-ranking officers during the war.

"Well, it pains me to say it, sonny, but I had to hear it secondhand." I had lowered the tone of my voice, but the intensity was still there. "Do you know how many years your mother aged when she heard about McCulloch being killed at Elk Horn? And her not knowing ary you were there with him or not.

"Rangers disbanded after that. Lost their leaders to the war and the Union." It saddened me to say it and they knew it, for next to Cora, my one true love had been riding for the Texas Rangers. At one time I thought my sons shared that same zeal. I reckon I was wrong.

"And you," I said, turning on Chance now. "You ain't gonna be outdone by your little brother, so you take off to find some Union outfit and see can you find him and kill him ary you come across him."

"That ain't true," Chance said, beginning to seeth as he spoke.

"The hell it isn't!" I blurted.

"I fought for the Union, damn it!" Chance countered with just as much vehemence.

"And I fought for Texas," Wash added with pride.

"Fools, the both of you!" I all but screamed in their faces.

"Watch it, Pa," Chance said in a hard, mean voice. "I ain't used to getting talked to like that."

"Well, you need to be! Hell, boys, you don't owe nothing to the goddamn Union or the Confederacy! Nothing! If you owe anything to anyone, it's me and Cora, by God!" If the rage hadn't consumed me so, I could have cried as the words poured out of me now. I'd gone too far to stop now, they had to know it all. "That woman gave you the best upbringing you could ever have gotten. You owed it to her to be here." I smacked a fist into the palm of my hand. "You should have been here when the murderous bastards came! Damn it, you owed her at least that!"

My words shocked Wash at first, but it was Chance who was the one who was taken aback. If he was a raging bull, I couldn't have waved a redder flag at him, for he was ready to charge me.

"Go ahead, *pilgrim,*" I goaded him, "you come right at me and I'll take every tooth out of your head, I swear I will!" The words, or maybe the look in my eyes, calmed him some and he settled for standing there with hands on hips, looking as tough as he thought he was. After a moment of exchanging stares, it was Chance who spoke up.

"No, you can't do it, Pa," he said through gritted

teeth, feeling as put out as I did, I imagine. "You can't blame me and Wash for what happened to Ma. You can't blame us for whoever it was that killed her. No, damn it, *no!*"

But his words only filled the fire within me and I told him the rest of the story. It was the worst part of that day and it truly tore at my heart, or what was left of it, whenever I thought of it. I hadn't experienced anything like it in my life, hoped I would never have to do it again.

"You *fool!* You *idiot!*" I raged in a voice that I was sure could be heard the next county over. "They didn't kill her! *I did!*" There, I said it. God, but it made me sick.

I hadn't seen a look on their faces like they had now since the first time I had slapped either of them way back when.

"You did," Chance said in an unbelievable whisper.

"Good Lord, what happened?" Wash mumbled, not even sure he was saying it, I'd measure, from the look about him.

Suddenly the rage was gone and all I could feel was sorrow; all I could see and hear was my Cora. I stared out past my boys into a land of nothing, but it was all there before my eyes, burned into my memory as permanently as though etched by a branding iron.

"Your ma proved to be more of a fighter than I reckon we figured her for," I said and this time it was me who was whispering, speaking slowly as I remembered what I could only have imagined that day I came back to her. "She always told me she couldn't shoot worth spit, she did, but she did right well with that old Navy Colt's I left on the fireplace. Yes sir.

"There was three of 'em head shot and dead and lying on the front steps of the house when I got here. I

59

reckon Cora was scared to death, but she done well with what she had. She must've shot one more inside the house before the fire was too much for her and she rushed out." I walked over to the spot where I'd found her lying there, screaming senselessly, her eyes bulging with fear like I'd never seen before. It was perhaps twenty-five feet from the doorway to what once was our ranch house.

"I make it she got this far before they grabbed her," I went on. I said it slowly, Chance and Wash hanging on every word. I sniffed some, wiped my nose with the sleeve of my arm, then pulled out my kerchief and blew my nose. "Then they had their way with her. She told me it was a dozen of 'em, but she could have been exaggerating. She was a gentle woman, your mother, that she was. I don't know what all they did to her, but it was enough to drive her out of her mind. She only recognized me once. The rest of the time she was out of her head, begging 'em not to do it anymore, seeing only what they'd already done and not knowing any peace.

"She was scared to death and out of her mind and not making any sense at all. Pain is what she was in. Truth of the matter is, I couldn't stand it. Couldn't stand to see her like that. Finally, she couldn't stand it either. Begged me to give her peace." I paused, slowly shaking my head in what would always be my darkest memory. "So I did."

Chance glanced at the makeshift grave. "I'm surprised the wolves and buzzards ain't pushed aside the rocks and dug her up yet."

Chance must have thought I was madder than a hatter when he saw that devilish smile cross my face.

"You wouldn't have wanted to be around me that day, boy," I said. "I got mean as could be." The smile broadened. "Found some strychnine that survived the fire. Drug them bodies a ways from the fire and poured a cupful of poison down the gullets and splashed it across the bodies of those fellers. I expect that if you look about, you'll likely find the remains of some dead wolves and buzzards. That's why them rocks are still in place.

"You'll have to excuse me, boys," I said, walking toward my horse and picking up the reins. "I got a need to be alone." I forked myself into the saddle.

"What about us?" Wash asked. "Why'd you bring us out here?"

"You two needed to know," I said. "About her." I nodded toward Cora's grave.

I pulled on the reins to go, thought better a moment and pulled the horse to a halt.

"By the way," I said to the two of them, still afoot. "It wasn't that scum you call Quantrill or that other fella Red Legs. This here was done by Comancheros."

Then I pulled my reins, dug in my heels, and left.

CHAPTER

★ 7 ★

The boys didn't make it back into town until late in the afternoon. I'd like to think they were paying their own bit of reverence to Cora, maybe even praying like their mother taught them to do on occasions like this. When they got back they didn't say and I didn't ask, so we let it ride.

I had meant what I'd said about needing some time to myself, but it wasn't to mull over what I'd done to Cora. No sir. I'd never forget what had happened to her, what I'd done to her at the very end of her life. I wasn't sure how long I could stand to carry that kind of guilt. But like I said, it wasn't Cora that was weighing on my mind now. It was the boys.

Ever since they had returned I'd had a gnawing feeling in my gut, a feeling that was hard put to describe but an unpleasant one to be sure. It was bothering the hell out of me too. At least it had until I'd gotten out to the ranch house and Cora and spilled my guts to the boys, let them know what and how I felt. It was then that I'd picked up on that feeling, then that I knew the god-awful truth about what that feeling really was.

It was when I got back to town and reined in up in front of Margaret's boarding house that it finally struck me. It was past the noon hour but I knew I could count on Margaret to give me at least a cup of coffee, if not some leftovers from her noon meal. I'd be lying, hoss, if I didn't admit to wanting someone to listen to me right then too. Margaret seemed to know more about me than I knew my own self, so I knew I'd get a sympathetic ear.

"You took them out to the house, didn't you?" she said when I removed my hat and took a seat at the almost bare community table. The way she said it, it was more a statement of fact than a question. I reckon the sad look on my face said most of what she saw. And if she was seeing a mite of despair, well, she wasn't far from accurate.

"You need something to eat," she said when I didn't answer. It almost made me smile. I never have been able to figure out why a woman's answer to the problems of the world is a square meal. Maybe it's designed to make you take your mind off of what's bothering you until the she-lion feeding you can come up with an answer her own self. At times like these I knew it was more a distraction than anything else, but I'd also gone without a decent meal more often than I cared to think about, so I was always ready for one when offered. I sat there sipping my coffee and trying to concentrate on what was suddenly a gigantic problem in my life. Trouble was, I wasn't having one whole lot of success at it at the moment.

Rachel was trying to cater to the wants and desires of some spiffy, thin as a rail drummer passing through town, who had taken up a seat at the opposite end of the community table. Rachel was patiently reading off the list of what she had on the menu for that meal, but her customer was acting as finicky as a newborn with the colic.

"Boiled beans," he groaned. "They would give an ostrich indigestion at this time of day."

"Well, sir, you could try some bacon," Rachel said, indicating a plate only half-filled with the thick crisp strips.

"Nothing but grease, grease," the pilgrim groaned, a sickly look coming to his face now.

"There's corn bread," Rachel continued. "We always have plenty of that."

"My dear lady, I am not an Indian or a mule," the man said in a high-toned voice. I never could figure out how these back east folks could look down their nose at you while they were seated and you were standing, but I have to admit that this pilgrim was doing a mighty fine job of it on Rachel now, who was almost in tears. Fact of the matter was, he was starting to get on my nerves.

"Then, damn it," I said in a loud, clear voice that mixed no words, "help yourself to the mustard! But for God's sake, *shut up!*"

"Well, I never!" the man said, taken aback.

"Part of the country you come from, they likely don't at all. Only explanation for the population thinning out in those parts, I reckon," I said with a growl that dared him to say anything else to me. I

64

must have been getting good at offending people that particular day, for the man looked like Aaron Burr had slapped him across the face and challenged him to a duel that very minute. Only this fellow wasn't much more than good at running his mouth, so he picked up his things and made a quick exit, which suited me fine.

"You pass me that bacon and get some more of that corn bread, darlin'," I said to Rachel with a wink, "and don't fret none 'bout flannelmouths like that one. Your cooking's too good for 'em anyway." The words perked her back up some, and I have to admit that I was feeling a mite hungry then.

Margaret brought out a small bowl of stew and set it down before me. Then she took a seat opposite me, coffeepot in hand, and took to watching me make quick work of putting away the stew, bacon, and corn bread in no time. My coffee cup was never empty, nor its contents cold. There are days a man can't ask more than that.

The meal was fine and I said as much to both Margaret and her daughter when the two of them were in the room, but once my mind was off the food, I still had to face up to what I was sure was going to be a major problem in my life.

"You *did* take them out to the house, didn't you?" Margaret asked.

"That's a fact, ma'am," I said.

"And none of you took it too well, I gather?"

"Right again." There was silence as I drank more coffee and Margaret poured more. I reckon she figured I was going to be the one who opened up to her and would do it in my own time. Like I said, she gave me the impression she knew me better than I did.

"I think I lost 'em, Margaret," I finally said for

openers. She frowned and I continued. "The war changed 'em. I told 'em what I thought about the war and them going off to it."

"And?"

I felt myself flush before I spoke, for I knew that what I would admit to next was far from right and it was embarrassing to say so. "And I blamed them for Cora's death," I said softly.

"Oh, Will, you didn't." Margaret suddenly had my free hand in her own, squeezing it as though she could transfer some sort of energy to me in the doing of it.

"I'm afraid I did," I found myself saying as I looked back at her. "And you know something? I don't think I've ever seen Chance look at me in such a hateful way as he did this morning. Don't know if I could stand to see that look again. I really don't."

Slowly, I pulled my hand away from hers.

"Margaret, Cora ain't but a few days gone," I said in what must have seemed a bothersome tone. Or maybe I was simply more aware of my wife's death than most.

"I know, Will," she said, almost apologetically. "If you think back, why, you and Mr. Ferris changed a mite from the time you went off to fight those Mexicans back in '46 and the time you came back."

"I won't deny it one bit, Margaret, but when we came back we had a whole new belief in freedom and being able to do as we please because we *fought* for it."

"But think a minute, Will," she continued. "Isn't that just what Chance and G.W. did? Haven't they earned their independence, their right to be looked at as grown men, instead of just the boys of Will Carston? They finally had a chance to prove themselves and they took it when they went off to war. Don't you see, Will, they've come back *alive* and you can't take that away from them. They've proved they can survive a war, just like you did.

"The war changed everyone, Will, even you." She smiled at me in that happy way she had. "Times are changing, Will."

Maybe she was right. Maybe times were changing. Maybe I was just too damned old and stubborn to see those changes, much less accept them.

Even during our years as rangers before the war, Chance and Wash had always been "Will Carston's boys," just like Margaret said. But they had gone off and fought a war, all by themselves, without Will Carston there to help them along. I wasn't sure what kind of scars they had, but they had come back alive.

Maybe things had changed and Chance and Wash no longer needed me. As a father it was a hard fact to accept, for as much as I'd cussed them and told them how worthless they were, there was still something inside me that said I needed them something fierce.

CHAPTER

★ 8 ★

Like I say, Chance and Wash didn't get back to town until late in the afternoon. By that time Margaret had bolstered my spirits more than they'd been in a considerable while, but that didn't change what there was between me and my boys. Margaret may have pointed me in the right direction and given me some advice I was too stubborn to otherwise see, but that didn't mean my boys had the same ideas. No sir.

I reckon that's why when they did get back to town, the boys and me just sort of played it like a mongoose staring down one of those big-time boa constrictors I'd read about in the science books. You know what I mean, peaceful coexistence is what I reckon you'd call it. If you get my drift.

They ate their evening meal at the Porter Café and I

had mine with Margaret and Rachel and their guests. I figured me and those boys of mine needed a mite of cooling off, so I was purposely staying away from them. Hell, they each had enough gumption to light into me like so much lightning going through a gooseberry patch and I don't mind telling you that that is one hell of an experience, son.

I woke up the next morning to the sound of those axes pinging away at the deadwood Margaret had persuaded her customers to gather for her. From what I'd seen of my boys' ability to make quick work of it the day before, I'd say she had nominated them as chief ax wielders. Looking out on them that morning as the sun was just rising, I felt that same mixture of pride and well-being I'd felt when I first saw them the previous day, swinging away like they were. I reckon there's something in a man that swells up and won't let go when he sees his boy grown up and doing a fine job of the things he did so long ago. I could remember the look on my daddy's face when he saw me working as hard as I could at a man's work around the house to try to impress upon him my skills as a man, little as they were at the time.

I sloshed some water in my eyes and gathered my razor and shaving material before making my way downstairs and out back where Margaret kept hot water on the boil for early morning shavers like me. I've got to tell you, hoss, walking out back was more than a project for me that early morning when I stepped through the back door and realized that Chance and Wash had those long handled axes in their hands and weren't swinging them at deadwood. The way I figured it, why, if they hadn't had any coffee yet, they might just take to tossing one of those axes at me simply for the pure hell of it.

"Morning, lads," I said in as cheerful a manner as I knew how.

"Right," Chance said and went back to swinging at deadwood.

"Yup," was all I heard from Wash as he did the same.

From then on, I sort of got ignored until Margaret called us in and set us down before larger than normal portions of ham, home fried spuds, biscuits, and a center plate filled with scrambled eggs.

"Looks like you're fixing to feed a condemned man his last meal, or someone who ain't been fed in some time," Chance said to Margaret.

"Well, you're going, aren't you?" Margaret said to anyone who would answer. "The three of you?"

"Wash," Chance said with a growl.

"Never said a word." His younger brother shrugged.

"Pa?" The scowl stayed there, but I ignored it. Margaret was too good a cook to let anything spoil a meal like this.

"Got me, son. Must be woman's intuition. I hear tell it's mighty strong on some things." When I gave a quick glance in the direction of Margaret, I saw the back of her neck get a tad red as her cheeks flushed the same color. Then she disappeared without a word, presumably for more coffee.

I think we stretched our eating time to all of fifteen minutes for that meal instead of the usual five. There was too much food and it was too good not to let your taste buds savor the portions as they went on down your gullet. It also gave a body time to think some more, and I had no doubt that the three of us men and the two women had our brains working right fast on just what it was we would say that morning, once the palavering began.

Chance was the first one to speak. "I saw Nathan Potts this morning," he said, pushing away an empty plate. "Asked him 'bout his signature and how he signs it. Showed me how he does it."

"Do tell."

"Sounded right proud when he added those three letters after his name. F.M.C. is what they were. *Free man of color* he says it stands for."

"That's a fact," I said, slowly finishing the food on my own plate. But secretly I had to admit to feeling a goodly amount of pride swell up in me, if for nothing else than the fact that, at the age of thirty-two, my boy was still listening to me and searching out the meaning of my words. I reckon it was also an indication that perhaps I hadn't lost them after all, perhaps Margaret was right in what she said. Seeing her smile at me with pride the way she was doing told me that she was feeling the same thing.

"He says you bought him from some fella not long after you settled this town, then gave him his freedom. Says he owes you a lot."

"Nathan Potts don't owe me nothing, son. That's the way I see it. I done him what he considers a big favor and he done us all a big favor in return by staying on as the town livery man. But you're right, I did buy him and set him free. Just about the time I brought your mother out here and she was carrying you."

"I think I understand what you were talking about yesterday, Pa," Wash said, finally taking part in the conversation. "About Nathan and all."

"Good," I said. "Then you hadn't lost your brains,

like I once suspicioned." I paused a moment, forked another piece of food into my mouth and glanced at my youngest son. "There's days I could swear you'd been dropped smack dab on your head way back when."

"No, sir." The boy smiled from across the table.

"Sure is a lot about the people and this town that I don't know," Chance said.

I looked Margaret in the eye when I said, "Seems to be a lot of that going around these days." The woman blushed. Me, I kept as straight a face as I could.

"I'm glad you enjoyed the meal," Rachel said, likely trying to get her mother out of a predicament. "Mother, why don't you get the gentlemen more coffee and I'll clear the table?" Suddenly, Margaret had a legitimate reason to leave the room and regain her composure.

"Chance, I'll get our gear and meet you and Pa over at his office," Wash said.

Margaret entered the room as Rachel and Chance were leaving it—Rachel heading toward the kitchen, Chance the front door. She had a bit of a scowl about her.

"You can be an embarrassing man, Will Carston," she said, busying herself with cleaning off the table.

"Speak for yourself, woman," was all I said in reply as I took my last gulp of coffee and rose from the table.

"I made some sandwiches for you and your boys, Will," Margaret said, setting three separate cloth sacks of food on the community table. "Ham sandwiches. I hope you like them."

"Well, now, woman, you served up a tidy amount of food this early in the morning for the Carston clan. Tell me, what are you gonna feed that finicky drummer when he gets up?" I asked with a smile.

"Boiled beans and corn bread," she said, smiling right back at me.

At the office I told Joshua to go have breakfast. Chance and I filled the time Joshua was gone with loading up extra cylinders for our six-guns, silence filling the room. The only bothersome thing was seeing Wash sitting there sipping coffee while his brother and I worked on our guns.

"Didn't them Dance Brothers make any spare cylinders for that piece you're wearing?" I asked. "This ain't a picnic we're going on, you know."

"Leaving town, are you?" Captain Alen said, appearing in the doorway. I'd left the door open to let in the cool morning air, but apparently we had eavesdroppers about. The sneer on the captain's face was making me like him less and less each time I saw him.

Wash was on his feet, a cross look on his face. "You know, mister, I *hate* the sight of that uniform."

"Easy, Wash," I said, for I knew the boy would kill the man in a minute if he wasn't held back.

"You'll have to forgive my brother," Chance said calmly. "He just found out his mother's dead and he's a mite on edge. Besides that, he's a hothead."

"That's tough," Alen said with as little compassion as I've ever heard anyone speak of the dead. "A lot of people died in the war. This is a hard land. You should know that." He paused for only a second as that superior sneer reappeared on his lips. "Leaving town, huh? I should have known you people didn't have any guts—"

Wash had the look of death in his eyes and I'm not talking about his own, son. But it was Chance who moved first. His gun wasn't close at hand, but he was closer to the captain than Wash or I and he made good use of those long legs of his. It only took two full strides to get to his full height and stand face-to-face with Captain Miles Alen. By that time, Chance had drawn his bowie knife and had it nudged up against the captain's chin, forcing the man back against the door to my office, a look of fear in his eyes.

"You don't understand, mister," Chance said, his eyes blazing with rage, his face only inches from the captain's. "She was *my* mother too, and I could not care less about the rest of the folks who died in the war. Fact of the matter is, I could cut your liver out here and now and feed it to you while you died, you filthy bastard." Miles Alen didn't like being talked down to any more than anyone else would have, but there wasn't a damn thing he could or would do about it, not unless he wanted to die an instant death. No sir.

"Ease up on him, son," I said, figuring I was about the calmest one of the four of us.

"What!" I'd purely flabbergasted Chance with my words.

"Oh, I wouldn't mind you killing him," I said in an even voice. "But hard as you're pushing, why, you'll likely send him through that plate glass he's backed up against. And I don't mind telling you, son, glass is hard to come by out here. Got that all the way from St. Louis, we did."

Chance eased off just a mite, but not before Joshua found himself stuck outside by the two men standing in the doorway. I've got to tell you, hoss, if there is one thing Joshua has, it's a sense of humor that is about as dry as the desert.

"If you're aiming to skin him, Chance," he drawled, "I can have his hide tanned and cured by the time you fellers get back. Meat's likely poisoned though. I'll just spread it around my wolf traps and kill off a few more of them varmints."

"Don't forget the ears," Wash said from inside. "Nail 'em up above the doorway with a patch of that blue uniform to let 'em know what happens to his kind down here."

Fun was fun, but the words had only given Chance an encouraging look that said any second now he was going to slit the man's throat.

"Put it away, Chance," I said, getting up and strolling over to the captain. I could see that it pained Chance something fierce to put that knife away, but he did. Captain Alen, well, he wasn't out of deep water yet. I took over the very spot Chance had stood in and now it was me talking down to the man.

"Captain, you started this day off in a bad way, but it was your own choosing. Next time you run your mouth to either of my boys, I'm not gonna hold 'em back. I hope you understand that."

He nodded slowly, getting some of his color back.

"Second thing you've got to understand is that me and my boys ain't running from nothing. It's true what they say about their mother being dead. And we're going after the ones responsible for it. We'll get 'em too. I've no doubt about that, for these two boys ain't never run a day in their lives.

"Simple truth of the matter is, Captain, the three of us are gonna be coming back, and I don't want to see nothing in this town changed any different than it is now. Like I said before, you want to stay in town with your men, you're welcome. You break up any of my St. Louis glass or try taking over this place—" here I paused a moment, stroking my jaw as a man in thought would. Truth was I already knew what I was going to say, I just wanted this pilgrim to sweat about it some. I finished by speaking my piece to Joshua.

"He breaks up any of my St. Louis glass, Joshua, you do two things."

"Name 'em, Will."

"Skin this culprit alive and do just what you were speaking of: Cure him, tan him, and use his innards for wolf bait. I'll pay you five dollars a head for each one you kill.

"Then you find the lash-up this pilgrim is with in the United goddamn States Army and bill 'em for every piece of my St. Louis glass they bust up. This war everyone's talking about is supposed to be over, and I'll be damned if it's gonna start all over again in my town."

"You betcha, Will. Said, done, and did." Joshua nodded with pride. I knew he'd carry out my orders to the very word too.

I guided the captain by the elbow and quickly had him back on the boardwalk.

"Now, Captain, I don't know what it was beside making an ass of yourself that you come to see me about, but it's gonna have to wait until I get back. Me and my boys have got some snake hunting to do."

Captain Miles Alen had suddenly gotten his color back as he left. Fact of the matter was, his face was turning a livid shade of red as he stalked off.

CHAPTER
★ 9 ★

When I returned to the office, Chance was working his Colt's revolver in and out of the holster he had fashioned for himself.

"Ain't that just handy, now?" Joshua was saying. "Be right handy, won't it, Will?"

"I reckon." Fact of the matter was his six-gun would be in a lot more stable position than a lot of the cross draw holsters were. "Practice with it, why, the boy might even get good."

"Not hardly," Chance said with a good bit of pride. "I am good, Pa. What you mean is I might get *fast.*" One of the things I'd noticed in the brief time these boys had been back was that they didn't lack for pride in their abilities. No sir.

But I had to admit that Chance had indeed picked

up a new skill since leaving for the army. I didn't recall him doing all that much when it came to using buckskin or any other kind of hide. His mother had fashioned the shirts and britches for him while he'd been home. Maybe striking out on his own like that was proving a good experience for him after all. It was something to remember.

I studied the holster as we readied to leave. It was odd seeing a pistol on Chance's right hip, unnatural it seemed. Odder still were the two cylindrical bulges sticking out of the left side of the big black army belt that his holster now hung from. Side-by-side they looked like a grotesque growth that had taken root on the man's side, but a closer view proved them to be just what they were, two extra cylinders for the Colt's Army Model .44. I waited for Joshua to make some kind of comment, but he was as confused at first as I was. When he did recognize the forms, he only grunted.

"You fellers watch your topknot now," Joshua said when we mounted. "And don't fear 'bout these yahoos back here. Me and Nathan and the rest, we'll keep 'em in line. Best you can do is watch each other's backs."

"Good advice, Joshua," I said, nodding. I paused, frowned a moment, trying to remember something nagging at the back of my mind, and wound up reaching into the oversize buckskin jacket knotted over the back of my bedroll. "Almost forgot," I said, handing a badge to each of the boys. "You're deputies for now."

I could almost see a spark of excitement come to their eyes as they stared at the piece of tin in their hands. I knew what was running through their minds too. There was a day back before they'd both left for the war when all three of us had sported the badge of a

Texas Ranger. They were special days, those days. Back then we were . . . well, we were a family.

"These ain't gonna do no good where we're going, Pa," Chance said, the shine fading from his eyes. The look I'd seen had been nothing more than a fleeting reminder to him of things now gone, memories that were just that. Memories. I thought I saw the same look cross Wash's face. I do believe Joshua read the looks on our faces too just then.

"They ain't nothing like the old days, boys," he said, "but I got a notion your daddy's a-wanting to make sure these varmints know they ain't welcome back here or wherever Will Carston's gonna be wearing a badge."

Chance frowned before sticking the badge in his pocket. By the look about him, I'd a notion he was wanting to forget about the badge as soon as it was out of sight. Wash followed suit, motion, look, and all.

"Well, I'm glad to see you fellers are so excited about all of this," Joshua said, a mite put off by the boys' actions.

"Truth to tell, Joshua, I'm sick of killing." It was the first time I'd heard Chance speak out on the matter. "If it wasn't Ma that got killed, I'd tell you to go fight your own war. I've had more than my share." He finished his words by turning to look at me, likely to see if I'd get riled by them.

"This kind of thought-provoking conversation ain't gonna get us any closer to those Comancheros," I said, and wheeled my horse to head out of town.

We rode most of the morning in silence, north by northwest. I was out front and Chance and Wash were riding side by side some distance behind me, just as they had when I'd taken them out to the ranch the day before. I didn't know what they were thinking and didn't really care. All I knew was that it was my own thoughts that were consuming my mind that morning. Me, I was just a fixture atop my horse, who seemed to know more about what direction we were heading in than I did about them.

Whether they knew it or not, they had hurt me back there. I'd taken them out to the ranch to see where their mother had been brought to her death to get them fired up. I'd wanted to motivate them. I'd had the same thing in mind when handing each of them a badge. Give them a belief that we were doing things together again, that's what I'd wanted to instill in them. But I'd failed at it all and it hurt.

I knew that if Margaret had been there, she would have told me that I was wanting too much too soon, that the boys had just gotten back from the war. She would have been right too, but I'd missed them both while they were gone, missed them just as much as Cora had. Still, there were some things a man didn't do, no matter how much it hurt.

I thought a lot about that as we rode that morning. It made me wonder if women really knew how badly a man could be scarred in his lifetime. Did they ever realize the torment a man had to go through in his lifetime to remain a man? We had to be so damned tough and strong and never have an ounce of weakness, or at least if we did, we weren't supposed to show it. And if the Maker ever caught us crying alone in the night, why, he'd likely banish us all to hell and gone for showing it. Yes sir.

It wasn't until I pulled my horse to a halt for noon camp that I realized that Chance and Wash were just as much men as I was and likely had the same feelings.

Chance gathered up some deadwood, while Wash led the horses to a nearby stream for some water. Me,

I tossed a portion of coffee beans into the coffeepot and readied to make a small fire. This was all done in silence, part of which surprised me.

"Leastwise, you ain't lost your memory," I said, as the coffee boiled and we each gnawed at some jerked beef.

"Force of habit," Chance said from the side of his mouth.

It must have been scary for all of us, falling into that habit like it was yesterday. When we'd ridden as rangers, I'd made sure that the boys knew they each had an assigned duty when we broke for camp on those rides. We each knew that noon camp was a dry camp of sorts, with no more than coffee and a piece of hardtack to call food. You had to be ready to break camp right quick at times, and I wasn't about to give up my coffeepot and coffee beans. No sir. Why, there were times I could remember having coffee for an entire meal. I could also remember those good times we'd had back then. Fact of the matter was, I tried to bring them back now.

"Been a long time, ain't it?" Chance said.

"Times it seemed like forever," I said, remembering how lonely it had been around the ranch once these two birds had taken off for the war. "Rumors kept filtering in every so often. Heard at least twice that you boys was dead. Didn't know what to believe after a while. Your mother, she sure took up reading the Good Book on a regular basis. Aged her some, hearing those things."

"Things change," Wash said. Suddenly I noticed how cautious we all were about our words. In the back of my mind I was waiting for one of them to jump me, just as I was now certain they were thinking of me and each other.

"I've heard that, Wash. Yes, I have." I poured the rest of the coffee in our cups, sloshed the grounds on the fire, and stood up to finish my coffee. "Course, I also recall a fella saying that the more things changed, why, the more they stayed the same.

"I never quite figured out what it was he was talking about when he said that. Maybe he meant that war or no war, you two came back from it and I'm still your father and you're still brothers." I took a long swallow from the cup then tossed the remains onto the smoldering fire. "I don't know," I mumbled to myself as if no one else were listening, for the words weren't coming like I'd wanted them to now. The well had gone dry.

I rinsed out the coffeepot while the boys put out the fire, all in silence, just as it had been at the start. When we saddled up, Chance laid a firm hand on my arm before I could urge my horse onward.

"Maybe what he meant was you raised two sons who came back to the land they left, the family they left, when the war was over," he said. "Maybe he meant that those two sons didn't do nothing while they were gone but try to make you and Ma proud of 'em."

"And maybe they'd get around to telling you 'bout it one of these days ary you wasn't so god-awful cussed mean to 'em," Wash said.

"Maybe we'd best get moving," I said. "This sounds like another one of them conversations where I wind up on the losing end."

I didn't give them a chance to reply, only dug my heels into the flanks of my mount and urged it onward. I spent the rest of the afternoon staying right out front, the same as I had during the morning. The difference was that my boys had closed up on my rear.

Still, we rode in silence that afternoon, gaining a goodly bit of ground as we did.

I said nothing to them most of that afternoon. I planned on saying nothing to them that didn't have some kind of pertinence to the mission we were on now. Maybe they were right; maybe I'd jumped the gun too soon, demanded too much from them without giving them enough time to settle down. If that was the problem, then so be it. I would give them their wish.

It was during the middle of the afternoon, when the sun had reached what seemed to be a high spot of the day, that the two of them got suddenly curious.

"Pa?" Wash said.

"Yeah."

"If we're sticking our necks out like we are, wouldn't you say it was reasonable to ask about something we don't know?" He sounded cautious at best, reminding me of his younger days when he had a need to know something but was a mite scared to ask.

"What he's getting at but ain't saying," Chance said, not waiting for my answer, "is how come there's only the three of us going after these yahoos?"

"Finally started using your brain instead of your mouth, eh?"

"You said Ma claimed there was twelve of 'em. That's four-to-one odds against us," Chance said defensively. "Not that I've never gone up against them kind of odds before, but what about the town folk? Joshua and Nathan and the rest? Couldn't they have come along? Didn't they volunteer to help you once they found out Ma was killed?"

"Yes to all of 'em, Chance," I said. It kind of surprised me that they hadn't thought to ask about this particular subject yet. "Every man jack of 'em volunteered to ride out after them Comancheros once they found out your mother had fallen victim to them. Ary I'd let 'em, they *would* have come too."

"If you *let* them?" Wash asked in a voice as surprised as the look on his brother's face.

"That needs some explaining, Pa," Chance said with a voice that was suddenly as hard as the look on his face.

"Tell me something, boys," I said, addressing them both. "When the call went out for rangers, what did we do? What did you all do?"

"Saddle and ride," Wash said with a shrug. He was still confused about what I was getting at.

"That's right," I said. "Didn't matter if it was horse thieves or the whole Comanche nation. We'd saddle and ride." I chuckled to myself, remembering a time that seemed like way back when. "I remember a couple of times when we didn't know just what it was we were riding into."

"There's that," Chance nodded.

"How come it took you two pilgrims this long to ask about why there ain't more of us going on this trek?" Chance gave his brother a curious look, but Wash only shrugged. "I'll tell you how come. It's because whether you like it or not, you've still got the ranger in you.

"When I got ready to leave, you boys were right there, riding out with me."

"Yeah, but this is personal, Pa," Chance said.

"Damn right it is," I agreed in a hearty manner. "Hell, Chance, every time I went out as a ranger, I took it personal. Shoot, boy, stealing and killing and all is crimes against the state if ever there were any.

"But you know as well as I do that I never asked for any assistance unless it was from another ranger. That's why I told Joshua to stay in town while I was gone. It's why I told the rest of them I'd square this account on my own. It's also one of the reasons I had you two come along. No matter what that war did to you, I figured you'd saddle and ride.

"You see, boys, whether you like it or not, you're stuck with the past as much as you are with me. And you won't forget it any more than you'll forget that war you come back from."

They were silent after that, but I had a feeling for a while that afternoon that told me whether they wanted to admit to it or not, by God, these boys were still Texas Rangers.

We came to a shallow creek about sunset. There was enough water for the three of us and the horses, and that was fine with me. With a fair amount of dead-wood available, it was all the better. We each set about our tasks, as before, setting up camp and getting ready to eat the day's last meal. I knew where we were going next and took out Margaret's sandwiches. They had long since cooled off, but they would be as tasty as if Margaret had just made them.

"Some of the food they fed us was putrid, you know," Chance said around a mouthful of food.

"No. I didn't know."

"Tried putting it in tin cans, can you believe it?" he said in near astonishment. "Damn stuff rotted by the time we got it."

"Places we were, you had to furnish your own often as not," Wash said.

"This is the last we've got," Chance said as he polished off his sandwich and refilled his coffee cup.

"Don't worry, son," I said, holding my cup out to him, "we'll be picking up some more supplies about noon tomorrow."

Something clicked in Chance's mind then as some

85

of the pieces began to fall into place. When the answer came to mind, he cocked a daring eye toward me, a dark frown building on his forehead.

"Just where did you have in mind getting these supplies?" he asked.

I gave my son a brief smile before saying "Hell City."

You'd have to ask Chance just how the look on my face was, but I'm pretty sure I smiled when I saw him mutter "Damn" as his fist rolled up into a hard ball.

CHAPTER

★ 10 ★

Hell City was one of those lawless towns that had been around since before the war and would likely keep going on whether there was a war on or not. Hell City wasn't its real name either. Come to think of it, I'm not sure anyone knew what the real name of that town was. I reckon it was simply that you always came away from the place with a pure belief that it was hell on earth you were leaving. Let's put it this way, hoss, the town wasn't dangerous, it was deadly.

Chance knew it too. He was already up the next morning when I opened my eyes. But at first I couldn't quite believe what I was seeing.

"Two gun man, are you?" I said, throwing my blanket aside and squinting.

"You get into the kind of war I was fighting, you find out right quick that there ain't enough gunpowder made or enough lead molded to keep you alive," he said with what I thought to be a crooked smile. He went on to explain how he had found one of those pony express riders mochilas and cut it down some so he'd be able to carry the saddlebag on the back of his mount rather than in the front of the saddle like the pony riders did with their mail.

"Thought I recognized something foreign on your rig the other day," I said, drawing on my coffee. Wash was just beginning to move in his blankets.

"No, Pa, I ain't a two gun man, not a-tall." This time Chance grinned as wide as could be. "I just taken to wearing two of 'em." Chance working a second Colt's revolver into the military holster on his left hip was what I had woken up to. "Hell, I got two more in them saddle bags." He continued to grin. "Navy Colt's and one of them old sawed-off Sheriff's Models."

"Expecting trouble, are you?" Wash said, rubbing the sleep from his eyes.

"You can say that again, brother. If I was you, I'd do the same." Chance was no longer smiling. Trouble was I couldn't figure out whether he was getting his ire up from the thought of going back to Hell City or the very sight of his younger brother and a portion of the Confederate uniform he professed to hate so much.

"Why don't you two just settle down and have some breakfast before you take to killing one another," I said when I saw fire in the eye of my young'un.

That we did and ate in silence. Most of the time I'd say that's how it's supposed to be. A body ought to be able to get up, shave, drink a good half pot of coffee, and get some food down his gullet first off in the morning so he can collect his thoughts and come alive. One thing I've noticed is that it gets god-almighty hard to take on the world on an empty stomach and a fuzzy brain. Always figured it for being one of the reasons armies attacked at dawn.

"How come we're making a stop at this Hell City, Pa?" Wash finally asked once we got riding that morning. We were letting the horses have their heads, letting them take us at their own pace. Even at an easy lope, I knew we would be in Hell City by noon at the latest.

"A number of reasons, son. First off, we're gonna need a fair amount of supplies."

"But that ain't all," Chance muttered.

"Then we'll have to get your brother a decent meal. Ary you hadn't noticed, he doesn't fare well in the mornings on coffee and greasy hardtack alone."

"But that ain't all." Chance's voice was getting deeper, harder with each repetition.

"You know, G.W., I never had much to do with the Comancheros before your mother's death. Only thing I know about 'em is that we're riding in the general direction of where they hang out." I reined in my mount, swept an arm out in front of me to cover a vast amount of land. "They could be anywhere out front of us there. And it could take me forever to find 'em. But I ain't got forever, son. I got a town to tend to back there." I yanked a thumb over my shoulder to my rear.

"What he's gonna do, kid," Chance said, finally picking up on the conversation, although I suspicion he knew what I had in mind all along, "is the same thing you Johnny Rebs did during the war. He's gonna find someone just as bad as the ones he's going after and hire 'em to sniff out his counterparts."

I knew what Chance was talking about concerning the Confederates. In parts of Texas, the Confederates had made peace with some of the Indians and convinced them that they, the Johnny Rebs, were fighting the same blue belly Yanks the Indians were. Together they could do away with them and the Indians could have their own land back. In some cases it had worked, but the Indian soon found that he was no match for the better equipped Yank soldier and soon gave up the fight. Instead, he went back to overwhelming individual settlers on the Texas plains. Easier prey, I reckon.

"That true, Pa?"

"That's a fact, son."

"Then what's Chance so riled up about?" he asked, still curious.

I grinned, gave a sidelong glance at my older boy.

"Cause it's T. J. Faro I'm gonna hunt up."

"And who's T. J. Faro?"

"Before your time and none of your damned business," Chance said, spitting the words out like so much poison. It wasn't hard to see that T. J. Faro was some kind of embarrassment to Chance Carston.

"What's eating him?" Wash said, when Chance turned sullen and rode off ahead of us some.

"Running into T. J. Faro was one of your brother's more humbling adventures," I said with a chuckle. Then I proceeded to tell Wash the story behind Chance and T. J. Faro.

It had never been mentioned to Wash, even though he was only eight at the time. Chance was eight years older than Wash, all of sixteen, and yearning to be a man in the worst way. I was already a Texas Ranger and decided to put a badge on Chance, thinking maybe it would help him get over his desire. Hell, he'd been doing a man's work since he was all of ten or eleven. But you know how kids are; they don't consider themselves men until they can get into some kind of foofaraw and come out on top of the mess to boot.

I was chasing a man who had stolen some horses and tracked him and his mounts to Hell City, which is what it was called even back then. It was the first time I'd been there, knowing it only by reputation up to then. The town looked about as ugly and no-account as its occupants. I made the mistake of letting Chance pull his weight which, even though he was a growing boy, wasn't much compared to the toughs we encountered at the saloon the horses were tied in front of.

"Who belongs to those horses out front?" Chance demanded as soon as we entered the makeshift saloon. It was a dumb move, for he didn't even give himself time to adjust his eyes once we'd entered the establishment, just burst in and spoke up, bold as could be. Me, I stepped to the side as soon as I walked in, but Chance was standing right in the outline of the door, making himself one hell of a target.

"Well, now, ain't you the feisty young lad," a rough sounding voice said with a chuckle. It was T. J. Faro. He was big and bulky, rawboned and as rough looking as his voice sounded. The whiskers on his face hid part of a scar that covered his left cheek and led a small trail off back to his ear. It was a gruesome sight and made him uglier than he might have been. He wore a wide-brimmed sombrero and a vest that was decorated in the manner of a Mexican. I wouldn't have doubted it if I'd been told he had killed a Mexican for the vest.

"I said I'm looking for—" Chance started again, although I could tell he was regretting the action all ready.

"You just made a damn fool of yourself, stepping in

91

a doorway like that," Faro said. "Shoot, sonny, you could get killed standing there."

My own eyes had adjusted by now and I could see how troubled Chance was. He didn't want to back down, for he had his manhood at stake and me there watching every move he made. Yet, he still had some growing to do and looking up at T. J. Faro, who was a good six inches taller than him, wasn't the easiest thing he would ever have to do either. Chance was stuck between a rock and a hard place and didn't know just what to do about it.

T. J. Faro did something about it for him.

Faro squinted harshly for one split second, but I didn't think he was looking down on Chance when he did. Then he hauled off and hit Chance hard across the jaw, knocking him ass over tea kettle out the door and onto the dusty ground.

I heard a shot from outside, saw Faro's hat go flying off his head, and drew the Colt's Sheriff's Model I carried on my hip. It had a short barrel and was easy to get out when the need arose and this was one of those times.

Faro didn't budge when his hat when a-flying, meaning he was either fearless or stupid, or both. Instead he pulled his own pistol out and took quick aim with it. I could still see Chance's feet lying on the ground in the doorway, so I knew Faro wasn't shooting at my son, his aim being too high for that. But he'd placed himself in the middle of that doorway and was now the one who made an easy target for a back shooter. And, hoss, he was in trouble.

Two men had risen from a table, drawing their guns as they got to their feet. It was a cinch they weren't going to say hello to Faro, not from the look on their faces. I shot the first one in the center of his chest, was sure he was dead as he fell to the floor. The second one let out a shot that sent splinters flying from the door frame. I shot the gun from his hand then proceeded to shoot him in the chest also. He was dead before he hit the floor. Mind you, now, under any other circumstances I would have wounded both of them, but I had the distinct impression that you have to prove yourself once you walked into this town if you wanted to walk out alive. Laying out these two birds seemed about the best way to let the rest of these characters know where I stood.

"Looks like I owe you my life," T. J. Faro said and, holstering his gun, introduced himself and offered a hand. I don't mind telling you I was reluctant to put my piece away. I told him who I was and who the youngster getting up off the floor was. He chuckled as he gave Chance a hand getting to his feet. "And you owe me your life, sonny," he said.

"How's that?" Chance mumbled, feeling his jaw as he spoke.

"Your horse thief is out in the street," Faro said to me, ignoring Chance, an action my son didn't like one bit. "He must have snuck out the back when you come in the front. Was gonna back shoot your boy here if I hadn't put him on the floor."

"I'm obliged."

Faro chuckled again. "Not half as much as I am," he said, glancing at the two dead men in the saloon.

We rode out of town with the stolen horses, not having to watch our backs. T. J. Faro had guaranteed us safe conduct out of town.

"And you've never been back?" Wash asked when I had finished my story telling.

"Nope. But I'll tell you what, son. I'm gonna take T. J. Faro up on his offer. He might have to get rid of the dust, but if he's as honorable now as he was then, I'm gonna bring his memory up-to-date."

"But what about him being a bad man? It sure sounds like he was one."

I looked at Wash from my saddle, seeing another son growing before my eyes and wondering if what I'd taught him before he left home was equal to what he'd learned in the war.

"Son, being bad is reputation. It's what other people think of other people. Being honorable is like a man's character. It's what you are, what you feel in another man. Reputation ain't much more than looks you can change at a moment's notice. Honor won't leave no man once he's showed it."

"I see," Wash acknowledged.

"Besides," I added as an afterthought. "I got a notion T. J. Faro knows enough about Comancheros to find us the one we're a-looking for."

CHAPTER

★ 11 ★

Chance was checking his loads about a quarter mile from the outskirts of town when we caught up with him.

"Still as ugly as the first time," he said casually as he holstered his second gun and looked down on Hell City.

"You got a good memory, son," I said. "Don't reckon I'll forget that day either."

"Pa," Chance said in a menacing tone, a tad of red forming on the back of his neck as he gave a quick glance at Wash.

"Secrets out, Chance. He knows all about it," I said in an even voice. "But Wash ain't got nothing to say about it, have you, son?"

"No, sir," the fair-haired youth said, but couldn't seem to hold back a snicker. The sound didn't do anything but get Chance that much angrier than I knew he already was.

Well, son, that tore it.

"You two *pilgrims* listen up, you hear? You're gonna have to stop egging one another on like this or you won't be worth spit to any of us when we meet up with these Comancheros. Chance," I said, my glare bearing down on my oldest boy, "what happened was a long time back, and as I recall you learned something that day that set you in the right direction. I never shoved that mistake down your throat cause I figured it was more a lesson to be learned." I tossed a thumb in the direction of my far side, since I had one of them riding on each side of me. "Wash ain't gonna make light of it either."

Turning to Wash my glare was none the easier. "And you ain't gonna make light of it either, *sonny*. First off, it *was* a long time back. And second, there's a whale of a lesson to be learned in that story I told you a while back. You want to be grateful for it too, cause you don't have to go through it now." I winked a knowing eye at Wash. "You keep that in mind ary you think on making fun of it, for you'll have two Carstons to answer to. Understood?"

"Yes, sir," Wash said in a more somber tone.

"Chance?"

"You made your point." The furrow that looked as though it had been made by a Missouri mule was gone, so I knew I'd gotten across to the man.

"I don't know about you boys," I said, pulling my Henry from its scabbard, "but I always figured on going to these sort of conventions in a ready manner." I jacked a round into the chamber and set the hammer down easy as I lay the rifle across my saddle.

"Yeah," Chance said in agreement, pulling out his

own Spencer and checking its loads. "Know what you mean."

"Don't want 'em to get the idea we come to dance." Wash yanked out his Colt's Revolving Rifle and began putting caps on the somewhat odd looking killing machine.

"Watch your topknot, boys," I said. Both nodded silently in understanding and we moved into Hell City like some sort of trio of bad men who had come to kill, and perhaps we had. Putting the fear of God into a body never did him no harm that I know of.

The city hadn't grown any since I'd seen it last over a decade ago. Nor had it gotten any prettier. Or maybe that was the clientele we saw as we rode through the city and stopped at the same saloon I recalled riding up to so many years back.

I walked into the drinking establishment the very same way I had when Chance and I had come looking for that horse thief, stepping to the right and pressing my back to the wall as soon as I was in. Chance and Wash had the good sense to do the same to the left side of the entrance. They must have known we were strangers, for it got awfully quiet all of a sudden.

"I need something wet," I said as my eyes focused.

"Warm beer's the best I can do you," I heard a somewhat familiar voice say from what I thought to be the other side of the bar.

I squinted as my vision came into focus now. Then I smiled about the same time he did. T. J. Faro was just as grizzled as the last time I had seen him, although he might have put on a pound or two. Hell, he was about the same size as me and I'd be lying if I said I hadn't put on a couple of pounds since way back when.

"Still ugly as a snake in the grass, T.J.," I said. I leaned against the bar, feeling a mite more secure after seeing my old friend, if friendship is what we had entered into back then.

"Speak for yourself, Carston." I felt a hearty slap on the shoulder as Faro set a beer before me. "Looking fit, you are."

"You haven't changed either."

Faro let out an uproarious laugh. "You're a good liar too."

Chance and Wash leaned on the bar not far from me. Still, Faro knew they'd come in with me. He set two more beers down on the bar and took to studying the boys. He shook his head after going over Wash. Chance was a different story. He cocked a suspicious eye at Chance then squinted, drawing a picture in his memory and trying to pull out the right name to go with the picture. A spark struck a light and his eyes opened wide. "Oh, yeah, you're the young kid who come with Will the last time."

"Ain't young anymore." Chance wasn't acting any too friendly, but then, he had his reasons.

T. J. Faro snapped his fingers. "That's right! You owe—"

"I ain't forgot, mister," Chance interrupted the man. "Believe me, I ain't forgot."

"These are my boys," I said in passing.

"Boys! Boys? You mean he was—"

"Young," I said before a fight started.

"Yeah," Faro said, calming down. "Still cocky too." He smiled. "A real rooster, Will."

I had a notion T. J. Faro was seeing in Chance's eyes the same thing Captain Alen had seen in Chance's eyes a couple of days ago when we had left town. I was also pretty sure that, like Alen, he didn't like it one bit. No sir, not one bit.

The beer was warm, just as T.J. had promised, but it

was a taste a whole lot different from the rancid branch water we'd come across in more than one stopping on our journey, so we didn't complain. It occurred to me all of a sudden that it was awful quiet in the saloon, almost as though everyone had his ears perked up and was listening for whatever it was we Carstons were going to palaver about. T.J. noticed it too and had an uncomfortable look about him as well, something I didn't think would bother him after being in a place like this so long. But it did and that was bothering me. If you know what I mean.

"Say, Will, are you still—"

"In a manner of speaking," I replied, knowing he was wanting to know if I was still a Texas Ranger. I had thought over what Chance had said before we left town and had turned my badge inside out so it was facing the inside of my shirt pocket now.

I took a sip of the beer and studied Faro my own self. He was still wearing the Mexican-style vest and, although he was working the other side of the bar, I had noticed his sombrero hanging on the wall in the corner. His hairline was receding and the scar on his cheek was no longer as bright and noticeable as when I'd first seen it, but it was still T. J. Faro I was looking at.

"Fact is, me and my boys are on a mission of our own," I said and proceeded to tell him the whole story about Cora and how she had died. I left out the part about how she really died, at my own hands, with my own gun. I didn't want to have to discuss that with anyone but my boys, and I'd already done that.

"Something about it struck me as being a Comanchero type of raid," I said after relating the story. "That was several days ago, so I reckon the trail's kind of cold by now. I've been going over in my mind who I

99

could get to help me find these varmints, then you came to mind.

"What I'm wondering, T.J.," I said softly, "is whether you meant what you said about asking your help if I needed it. Well, I'm needing it now, and I'm asking it as well."

"Well, I . . . I . . . do you know how long ago that was?" I don't think I've ever seen anyone as flustered as T. J. Faro was right then, including my boys. "You've got to have a helluva memory to go back that far."

"Not really," I said. "I just put a lot of stock in the man who spoke those words to me."

His face changed from a look of surprise to doubt, a look that didn't know whether to stand fast or cut and run. On the other hand, he'd also just gotten a boost to his ego. I wasn't the only one who saw the confusion of the man.

"Pa mentioned something to me about you being an *honorable* man, on our trip up here," Chance said, raising an eyebrow that raised a question as well. "I had some deep concern about that statement then and I'm beginning to have more concern now."

"The only concern you're gonna need, mister," a voice from the back of the saloon came, "is getting out of here alive. T.J. ain't going no place." The man came out into the light, dim as it was. He was of medium height, a darkly tanned man with the kind of squint that comes from many hours of working in the sun. Whether he was a brush popper or a working cowhand, I didn't know. All I could tell you was that he thought he was dangerous.

Now, friend, it wasn't quite noon when we had ridden into Hell City. The saloon didn't have but three or four early morning drinkers in it when we entered. I didn't recall anyone entering or leaving after Faro had brought us our drinks, so I figured that what I was looking at was what I had to deal with. Unless, of course, there were a couple more of these surprise yahoos by the back door, and in a town like this that wasn't out of the realm.

A couple of gents who had been nothing more than spectators were pulling their chairs back from their tables, although none had gotten out of their chairs yet. That made it hard to tell whether they were going to remain spectators or take part in the ball when it opened.

"I don't think I like you," Chance said, getting downright mean about the way he was being talked to. Not that I blamed him, you understand. I was fixing to say the same thing.

"You don't want to do this, mister," Wash said. "My brother's mighty fast with that Colt's of his. Take my word for it."

The distraction was all that Chance needed or wanted. The man who had come out of the shadows was paying attention to Wash who was to the side of Chance now. Whether he was fast or not, Chance knew that when you get that close to a rattlesnake, you do unto him before he does unto you.

Chance did.

He wasn't all that fast. Of course, there hadn't been anyone to compare him to as far as a fast gun, except maybe Cullen Baker or Langford Peel. For being a fast draw, Baker wasn't much more than a loudmouth and a drunk who was good with a gun. The last I heard he had deserted the Confederate army and was wanted for a killing in Arkansas. Langford Peel had made a name for himself by killing a gunman named El-dorado Johnnie up Montana way, and was still up there for all I knew. But Chance did know how to point and aim while he shot from the hip. Surprise was what was on his side. Chance made it work for him. He drew his Colt's and fired, placing a slug high in the man's right shoulder, spinning him around as the man's gun went off and the bullet ricocheted off the ground.

"Drop it now or you'll go down with it," my boy said loud and clear, making his intentions known.

"Same thing goes for you, mister," Wash said, pulling out his Dance Brothers revolver and bringing it to bear on one of the one-time spectators in the crowd who had decided to take a hand in this fight. Wash was getting right handy with a six-gun too, I noticed. In making his move, he'd drawn his gun and maneuvered his body so that he was facing the men at the table. Whether he knew it or not, he was also standing shoulder to shoulder with his brother, Chance. "Got you covered, brother," Wash said in a calm voice.

A rush of pride ran through me then, seeing them standing there like that. By God, that's how I taught them to fight, back-to-back. By God, that was my boys.

But things weren't over yet, and neither was the talking. Another one of the yahoos had circled around to the front of the saloon and was about to pull the same thing one of them had tried the first time I'd come here. Let me tell you, son, you don't stay alive in this man's world by walking into the same trap twice, unless of course, it happens to be with a woman. In that case a man is dead meat anyway. When this fellow decided to take a hand in the game and stepped through the entrance, gun drawn, I made my presence known. From where he stood, he could easily have back shot both of my sons, but you can bet your bottom dollar that would never happen while I was anywhere around. In one motion, I cocked the Henry, brought it up to my shoulder, and plunked the blunt end of the barrel against this fellow's head. Real hard. I wanted his attention, but I think my words said just as much as that piece of cold steel setting against his brain.

"You drop that pistol of yours right slow, *sonny,* or I'm gonna splatter what little brains you've got all over the inside of this room," I all but whispered, as though the words were a secret between the two of us alone.

"He's right, Rye," Faro said in a commanding voice. "I'd never forgive you for making a mess of my place. Of course, you'd be dead, so that wouldn't matter, would it?"

I gave T. J. Faro a quick glance and saw a confident man standing behind the bar with a six-gun in each hand, ready to take on the very devil if need be.

"Now, boys, I've got a suggestion to make that I figure says it all," Faro continued, after a brief silence in which everyone held their stance, ready to kill or be killed. "This here's my place and nobody does any killing unless I say so. Hell, you kill each other off and I'll be left to clean the mess up, not to mention bury you fools. So you all put the hardware away and trade in your hard times for a drink on the house and then take a long walk to cool off.

"And while we're at it, let's get something else clear in everyone's mind." His voice grew deeper and harsher now. "I'm too damned old to be told what to do by anyone, *and I mean anyone.* And that, gentlemen, is that. Now, put the guns away."

I had a notion old T. J. Faro had served as a

sergeant in someone's army somewhere along the line in the rough life he'd lead, for I could recall Texas Rangers who were sergeants I had served with in the Mexican War who had sounded equally as gruff in their no-nonsense manner of speaking. Silently, if cautiously, we all began to lower our guns and put them away.

T. J. Faro quickly set to filling mugs of beer for those who bellied up to the bar, while Rye, the man I'd had my rifle on, crossed the room and proceeded to take care of his wounded partner. I noticed that Chance was the least trusting of the lot of us, leaning with his back to the bar, facing the man he had shot while he drank his beer. I had a sudden notion that a good sense of mistrust had gotten into my boys while they had been away at war. I also found myself understanding just how that could come about too. Fact of the matter was, I was feeling right strange at the moment. Hell, here I was a father and it was my boys who were teaching me lessons from life. Right strange, yes sir.

"I do believe I'll take you up on that request, Will," T. J. Faro said in a voice loud enough for everyone in the room to hear. "Man sits around on his duff long as I have, why, he'll get fat and old."

"Can't do much about getting old," I said, sipping my beer.

"True," he acknowledged, "but I reckon there're memories of the days way back when that'll keep old bastards like you and me taking to the trail every once in a while."

"Yeah, there's that." I wasn't about to make the man's decisions or push them on him, not after a fandango like the one we'd just been through.

"Besides, I ain't heard nothing said about me being

honorable in I don't know how long." I thought I heard a hitch in his voice as he spoke the words, and that might just have been a tug at a heartstring as well. You'd simply never get a man as big and tough as T. J. Faro to admit to it. "And I do owe you one."

"I understand."

"All right, you buzzards!" Faro yelled, "one more refill and this here bar's gonna be closed till I get back." He winked at me, smiled. "Give me an hour and we'll be on our way."

CHAPTER

★ 12 ★

T. J. Faro guaranteed us safe conduct out of town, just like he had the last time I'd come to Hell City. Just like last time, I had a notion we didn't get bothered because whoever did decide to go up against us would be going up against T. J. Faro, except this time it would be in the flesh.

I reminded T.J. that we were also in need of supplies, for I didn't figure on this trek being some weekend social or picnic. That didn't seem to bother Faro in the least, for he simply acknowledged my need and, when he was ready to go an hour later, produced a pack mule, complete with supplies.

It was the first time I had ever seen him outside of the saloon and I have to admit that he looked a bit more complacent than he appeared to be in the dark light of the saloon. His eyes were beady and black, cautious little things that were constantly darting around, taking in all movement within their range. The eyebrows were brown and as mischievous as they were bushy. Although his hair was thin and receding on top, his face sported a full beard that seemed both dirty and well kept at the same time, if that is possible. But then, life is full of illusions. The scar on his cheek, although fading from age, was still noticeable, a hint to anyone taking in the face of this man that they weren't dealing with some brand-new tenderfoot from back east.

But his face looked relatively peaceful and rested under the shade of his sombrero. A huge red bandana covered his throat and was tucked neatly down inside a simple cotton shirt. The Mexican-style vest and its decorative baubles were noticeable and shiny in the light. His trousers matched the vest, making me wonder for one brief moment if T. J. Faro indeed hadn't killed a man for the clothes he wore. He was capable of doing it, of that I was sure. If he was interested in killing, it would be done with the brace of Navy Colt's stuck in his waistband.

We rode out slow and easy, the four of us in line as we did. Wash and Chance were riding on the outside, each keeping an eye peeled to our rear. T. J. Faro and me, we just walked those horses out real easy like, trying to make an intense situation look as casual as possible.

"Think they'll miss you?" I asked by way of conversation on that long ride out of town.

Faro chuckled. "I doubt it. Nor will I miss them. These bandidos are no different than any other mortal. Once they have a few drinks under their belt, they stagger enough to make walking look like an art."

"Know what you mean, friend." I smiled. I'd seen

more than my share of men who had come under the influence of "Who-Hit-John" and suddenly found their legs to be a burden to them.

When we were well out of town we rode in pairs, following T. J. Faro in the north by northeast direction I figured he would take us.

"I did some asking before we left town," he said after we'd ridden a while. He spread a hand out to cover the entire expanse of barren land before us. "The Comancheros ride throughout this land. Throughout. But the ones I think you want, I think they are in this direction." His hand shot forward like an arrow, pointing in the direction directly ahead of us.

"You're my scout. If that's what you say."

We rode in silence that afternoon, stopping only toward sundown when we found good water to camp near. In this part of Texas it got hotter and drier than normal during the summer months, so taking better care of your horse than yourself was most often the rule out here. That meant a decent amount of good water and feed on a daily basis, along with a good rubdown at day's end. I knew that this would be only the first of a number of days in a land where water could be impossible to find if you didn't know the lay of that land, so it was imperative that we take good care of our mounts, and I told the boys as much. They tended to the mounts while I searched out some deadwood and T. J. Faro unpacked the necessary supplies from his mule.

Within half an hour we had a good strong pot of coffee on the fire and thick pieces of bacon on the fry pan.

"I've only got biscuits to sop up the grease with," T.J. said almost apologetically when Chance and

Wash came to the fire. It was apparent they had done a fair job of horse tending, as sweaty as they were.

"Long as it's food and reasonably hot," Chance said, grabbing a coffee cup and plate. He flinched as he dipped a biscuit into the pan, feeling the bite of bacon grease spitting back at him. But I could tell by the look of satisfaction on his face once the food was on his plate that the effort had been well worth it. Wash was just as daring in obtaining his evening meal.

"How did you come by that name, Mister Faro?" Wash asked when we were through eating.

"It's wise not to ask too many personal questions out here, my friend," the big man said. "The man you speak with may be wanted by the law in the next territory."

"What's wrong with that? I ain't out to do him no harm."

"That is true. But he doesn't know that. And even if you told him, he likely wouldn't believe you. You see, he is a cautious man if he has obtained this wanted status in his life. So he can only look at you in one way. Like you are the law from that territory, coming to take him back."

Wash shrugged. "Well, maybe that's just the way they are in Hell City."

"Oh, no, amigo. It is like that when they come *in* to Hell City. I've seen more than my share of bandidos, men who have deserted the army because they wanted no more war, men from both sides of the war, just like you two."

"Except we didn't desert," Chance said, making it real plain that he meant what he said. "Never have, never will."

"Now the war is over, but a man's life is still his own," Faro said. Then, smiling at Chance, he added,

"You still got things you don't want to talk about, right?" The grin widened.

"If you're trying to see how far you can push before I get froggy, mister, you're doing a right fine job of it," Chance said with a growl. If I knew Chance, he was getting ready to jump then and there.

"Ah, but we are all friends here, right?" T. J. Faro spread his arms out to encompass the fire and those about it. "So I'll tell you." He paused a moment, poured more coffee as he did. But I didn't think he was all that thirsty. For my money, he was keeping a weapon handy in the form of a cup of hot coffee he could throw in anyone's face who tried to throw down on him. And Chance might be the one he was expecting it from the most.

"A man must be good at something," he continued, shrugging in what I'm sure he considered modesty. "I found a deck of cards easy to handle. In fact, I was very good with them." He sopped up more grease with his one remaining biscuit and took a healthy bite, nearly encompassing the entire biscuit in his mouth.

"And Faro was the game?" Wash asked.

"This is a smart boy you got, Will," Faro said before swallowing his food. "He catches on real quick."

"That's a fact, T.J.," I said. "They're both right smart." I had always had to watch out for situations like this, even when Chance and Wash were youngsters. Like most brothers, they got downright jealous of the other one when something good was said about him. That meant that if I wanted to avoid a fight when I was around them, I had to come up with something to make both of them feel good about themselves. It should have surprised me that these two were grown men now and still acting like kids when it came to things like this, but I reckon sibling rivalry is like that. Besides, after this many years, I was almost getting used to it.

"I got so good with the pasteboards that I found out it is not always good to be good, if you know what I mean." With coffee cup still in one hand, he used the other one to enhance what he had said by holding it flat in the air and shaking it back and forth some.

"Caught you cheating, did they?" That was Chance, always calling a spade a spade, especially when it came to cards.

"Oh, no, they *accused* me of it," Faro corrected. "I don't cheat. I don't water down your drinks. You always get the same kind of drink everyone else gets in my place." He said it with a measure of pride, but it was short-lived.

"What he means is instead of watering down just your drink, he waters down everyone else's drink too," Chance said. "That way he don't play favorites and he still gets ahead."

"What is wrong with this son of yours, Will?" Faro asked, the playfulness now gone, suddenly replaced by a harsh dislike that had crawled into his voice. "Is he looking for a fight, is that it?"

"Well, now, that's a good question," I said, turning my gaze to Chance. Hell, I could defend him all night, but he was a grown man now and responsible for what he said and did, so I figured I'd let him play this hand out by himself. After all, it was he who had bought into it, not me.

"I'll tell you what it is, Faro," Chance said, letting his meanness show. "I didn't like you back then and I don't like you now. I don't like your kind."

T. J. Faro set the cup down.

"You see this, Will? The young one only wants to

know about my name. But this one," he growled at Chance, "he wants to be the one who'll *bury* me! He looks at me like I'm one of those bandidos back in Hell City. He's got it in his mind that I'm gonna pull this bandana over my face and rob him of his valuables. Huh!" he said in disbelief.

I didn't know what was going to happen next. But it wouldn't be long before someone got hurt playing this game. Wash was purely fascinated by what was going on. Me, I was running through my mind what I was going to do about it if things came to a head. I didn't have to wait long.

The fire was dying down and the sun was close to setting now. But it was the fire in the eyes of the two men at my camp fire that had my attention now more than any sunset. T. J. Faro leaned forward, as though to get closer to Chance who sat across the dwindling fire from him.

"You want to know why I wear this bandana, amigo?" He had Chance's attention now as he yanked the red bandana aside to reveal a jagged, grotesque scar that ran over the top of his collarbone and proceeded down underneath his shirt and out of sight. As tough as he was, I thought I saw Chance flinch at the sight of the scar. "That's why, amigo! What you see up here," he continued, using his left hand to trace the scar on his upper cheek, "goes much further than my face." He had Chance leaning forward from his squatting position, fully attentive to the odd neckline of the man opposite him. And that did it.

"How did you get it?" Wash asked, amazed at what he saw.

Quick as could be, T. J. Faro had one of those Navy Colt's in his hand and it was pointed dead center at Chance's chest.

"I got good at something else, amigo," Faro said with a wicked sneer. "I got good with a gun. I could kill you right here and now." He cocked the gun and I knew he could do it, without a doubt I knew it.

"Put it away, T.J.," I said. I hadn't drawn gun or knife. Maybe I was used to being obeyed, used to being the law. But I suddenly remembered that I didn't have my badge on now, and I had a notion that even if I did, T. J. Faro wouldn't have cared, for out here a man was law unto himself.

"The man who called me a liar, he pulled a bowie knife on me and decided he wanted to cut me up as well," Faro said, ignoring what I had said. "But like I said, I got good with a gun too. He cut me from cheek to chest, but I killed him. He won't never do that again to anyone." Faro was slowly shaking his head back and forth. "You want to watch your mouth, amigo, cause next time I'm gonna kill you, too. Comprende?"

"Mister Faro," Wash said, "I'd appreciate it if you'd put that Colt's back in your holster, or wherever it is you got it from. He's a hardhead and tends to run at the mouth at times, but you gotta remember, Mister Faro, he's my brother. Besides," Wash added, "if you don't, you'll be dead as that liar you done in."

Slowly, T. J. Faro glanced to his left and saw the same thing I did. Ever so slowly, Wash had drawn his Dance Brothers revolver and was pointing it with both hands at Faro's head.

"I always taught 'em to say what they mean and mean what they say, T.J.," I said, "and I do believe he means it."

It was enough to convince T.J. to pull in his horns, at least for now. Both he and Chance sat back on their heels, although I doubt that their eyes ever left one another.

113

"You boys better turn in," I said. "You want to play hero, you'll have plenty of time once we catch up with those Comancheros. Until then, the next one of you gets froggy, you jump my way and we'll see how long you last."

Everything else was done in silence that night as we tossed out our bedrolls and readied for sleep. The only conversation I heard was between Wash and Chance, and it was a short one.

"Looks like you're really running up a tab, Chance."

"How's that, Wash?"

Wash smiled in the night. "Shoot, brother, now you owe both Mister Faro *and* me."

"Damn," was all I heard Chance mutter in the night.

CHAPTER

★ 13 ★

We could have been sitting in a graveyard, it was that quiet the next morning. I was the first up, chucking more wood on the fire and getting a pot of coffee going. I reckon it was the smell of the coffee that wakened T. J. Faro, but it wasn't until I tossed some bacon on the fry pan that Chance came to. I swear that boy has a stomach that can only be equalled by a bottomless pit! Wash, well, I reckon he could have slept all day if Chance hadn't kicked him awake.

T.J. hadn't slept well the night before; I knew because I'd heard him toss and turn more than a tired man will. I reckon I'm just a light sleeper. It was seeing him shudder that morning as he swallowed his first gulp of my coffee that made me even more certain something was bothering him.

"Made it too strong for you, did I?" I asked. I've

tried to make a habit of starting off the morning with something good to say, but I'll tell you, hoss, ever since my boys had come back I was finding it harder and harder to do. T. J. Faro wasn't making it any easier.

Faro spit to the side, mumbled something to himself and spent the rest of the morning in silence. He had a bur under his saddle and it was bothering him something fierce.

Me, I had my own problems. I'd woken up with a sudden urge to get on with it, to find those heathens and get on back to town. I reckon I was experiencing what my boys must have gone through during the war, the impatience of waiting for something to happen. Any man who goes off to war can tell you about it. It is waiting that gives you the gray hair and makes your blood run cold. Once you get into actual combat, you are generally all right, but when you have to sit on your bottom and wait for what you know to be inevitable to happen, well, it gives your mind time to pause. Time to think. That isn't necessarily the best thing for a body to do, either. Start to thinking and you'll get to doubting. Like I was that morning.

I was doubting myself as a father and as a man. Maybe that was why I wanted to get on with it and get the whole damn thing over with. I knew I had failed Cora. I'd left her at the ranch house when I should have known better. I'd failed by coming back to a woman who was stark raving mad, and who I wound up killing with my own gun. Now I was wondering if I wasn't failing my boys too. Oh, I was good at blaming them, but was I failing them too by leading them into what could be the whole Comanche nation and one hellacious band of Comancheros? Shouldn't I be out here my own self? Wasn't it all really my own fault?

After all, I'd been the one who left Cora alone. It really had nothing to do with Chance or Wash and their leaving for the war.

"Something wrong, Pa?" Wash asked as we mounted to leave camp.

"Whatever it is," Chance said, "these two got a case of it."

We rode hard that early part of the morning, trying to get as much ground covered as we could before the sun came up and took to frying us and the horses as well. You have to remember, friend, we were getting on in the summer and each day seemed to get that much hotter. And cover ground we did, but you can bet that by the middle of that afternoon we weren't looking for anything more than a water hole to make camp near. It was close to sundown when we finally found one.

The water was brackish and the quantity small, so we made the most of it, letting the horses have first go at it, filling up the coffeepot next, sparsely watering our own gullets last.

"This one can be hard to find," T.J. said in a parched voice. "I wasn't sure it was still here."

"Know this part of the country well, do you?" Chance asked.

"Know the country?" T.J. asked in astonishment, as though offended at even the thought of such a question.

"Better get used to men like T.J., Chance," I said. "Fellas like these, why, they know most of the lizards on a first name basis, all except for the younger ones, of course." T.J. laughed and again I knew I had averted a fight. Truth to tell, I was getting mighty tired of being some kind of a peacemaker between two men I felt certain would clash sooner or later. Mighty tired.

"Don't look like an awful lot of water, T.J.," Wash said, taking in the water hole.

"Wait until morning·to fill your canteen," he replied. "Mother Nature works in mysterious ways. You will see."

That was about as talkative as any of us got until after supper that night. Of course, it wasn't Chance or Wash that struck up the conversation. I had a distinct notion that the well had gone dry when it came to words for my boys. It was T.J. who took to palavering.

"Your boys sure do know how to stir up a fuss, Will," he said, as though nothing had happened.

"Do tell," I said, not sure what he was leading up to.

"You ever do those things with your boys?" he said.

"Those things?" He had me confused. That took in a lot of territory.

"Hunting. Fishing. Riding. You know, things you always told your young 'uns you'd do with 'em and never quite got around to?" I couldn't tell whether he was happy or sad, mostly just reminiscent, it seemed.

"Oh. Yeah, sure." I scratched my jaw, thinking back. "Some. I reckon there's some I never did get around to. Yeah, I remember. Why?"

"I hadn't thought about him in years," he said, shaking his head and looking like he was in some other world. "My boy," he said when he realized that other world was just that, another world. "Never thought an old ugly like me could have one, did you?"·

"Nope," Chance said. "That's a fact."

I could see that he was on the prod to get T. J. Faro riled up again, but I wasn't having any of it, not tonight.

"Son," I said, in a voice that must have been a growl, "if you don't shut your mouth, I'm gonna have to gag you, and the only thing I got to do it with is one of my socks, and I ain't gonna tell you how long I've had it on. Now, *shut up!*"

"You should then, Will, you should." Again he shook his head in what seemed like disbelief. "Mine went bad on me. I used to wonder ary he'd have walked the straight and narrow if I'd done all that stuff with him back then. Give up on wondering after a while, but your boys got me to thinking on it again. Yes sir."

"Huh?"

"What's he talking about, Pa?"

My boys were just as confused as I was. The man was talking in riddles. Then I thought for a minute and a few things began to fall in place. They were ugly as sin if they were true, but it all began to make sense in a bizarre sort of way.

"I don't think Mister Faro's gonna do you any harm, boys," I said slowly, "not if I'm right."

"Pay attention to your daddy, boys, he's a smart man," T.J. said with a wink.

Chance and Wash frowned at me in silence, but I threw the frown right back at them. Let them do their own thinking. Besides, I had a hunch T. J. Faro was wanting to talk now, tonight, so he could get it off his chest. At least, what it was he had to say. Me, I won't stop any man from saying his piece.

"Used to take fishing for granted, I did." He had his sights set on some far off star now, reaching back to that dream he never did have. Who he was talking to I didn't know, but it was the kind of talking that was for listening, I can tell you that, son. So I gave him the courtesy and hoped my boys would do the same. "Treated it like some chore the two of us had to do. Never did talk to him though. Nor when I went hunting.

"Odd, for he never did talk to me back then. But then, I reckon he was a mite feared of me too. Back then, in his youth." He was silent for a while, thinking some more, I reckon. Maybe seeing him too.

"Know what you mean," I said after a while. "I been doing a heap of thinking about what I've missed with these two birds my own self. Makes a body wonder what it is he does right and what it is he does wrong."

"That it does," T.J. said, suddenly back in our world. "Well," he said as though having just embarrassed himself, "pass the rest of that coffee and let's call it a night." Reaching down for the handle of the coffeepot, I could have sworn I saw T.J. run a hand past his upper lip and sniffle as he did so.

"What about that son of yours?" Chance asked in his usual less than tactful tone of voice.

"Let it ride, Chance," T.J. said when he sat upright again with the cup of coffee in his hand. But there was something different about him now, something maddening about the voice and the face. Both were hard as could be and the beady little eyes were now as daring and dangerous as my oldest son's. And Chance didn't like looking into them one bit. No sir. "Let it ride."

They stared at one another for a minute or two, but they were long ones, I'll tell you that. I had the notion Chance was wondering when T.J. would pull his Navy Colt's, while T.J. was wondering when Chance would pull that bowie knife of his. Wash had his hand down by that Dance Brothers pistol of his, and I was snaking my hand toward my Henry. I'd like to think I spoke up first because I was the oldest and knew better than this type of child's play. The truth is, my nerves were starting to get to me.

"All right, children, let's stop the game playing," I

said, picking up the Henry and jacking a new round in the chamber, as though I were checking the rounds. "I don't want this to be some kind of nightly occurrence."

The remaining few minutes of daylight they spent moving around the camp like predators stalking one another, moving that slow they were. I didn't have to be told that the longer T. J. Faro and Chance stayed around one another, the closer they came to some kind of showdown.

When we rolled out our blankets, T. J. Faro was the only one to speak. He sounded as though he had calmed down considerably, as though he had passed a crisis and now it was all over.

"You take good care of these young 'uns, Will Carston," he said softly. "You don't know how good you've got it."

"If you say so, pard," I said and pulled my hat down over my head and my blanket up over my shoulder.

I was hoping he'd spoken his words loud enough for both my boys to hear them, especially Chance. If he heard the voice and the words, Chance would know what I was just finding out. Beneath all that gruff exterior and harsh words was a man who had a bit of good in him. Or, at least, a man who wanted someone to know that he had once had a good heart.

CHAPTER

★ 14 ★

I don't know about the boys, but T. J. Faro slept right peaceful that night. At least, if he tossed and turned, he didn't wake me up doing it. He was turning out to be a strange sort of bird, T. J. Faro was. Still, when I got up that morning and started the fire up again, I had a notion that old Faro had settled up some past due debts with himself the previous night. It continually amazes me how healthy talking can be sometimes.

"Not bad," Faro said upon taking his first sip of my coffee.

"Always does taste better when you don't have a sour taste in your mouth to begin with," I said, keeping an eye on him to see what his response would be.

"I reckon," was all he said as he proceeded to finish his first cup of the hot black stuff. Maybe it was possible that we'd have a normal day out of this expedition yet.

We started out early again, trying to outrun the morning heat and covering a fair amount of ground with our tracks. But T. J. Faro knew where he was going. By noon we'd come into the Pecos River and took to following it north and just a tad west. If nothing else we would at least have decent water for the horses, and after all, they were the ones doing most of the work when it came right down to it.

T. J. Faro got real talkative that afternoon, hot as it was. Of course, all he had to do was stop by the Pecos for water if he wanted to give himself or his mount a break. He started pointing out various landmarks and water holes as we made quick work of passing through the area. Me, I paid close attention to what he was saying. Like I said, old T. J. Faro was likely on a first name basis with all of the lizards in these parts of the country. And, son, if he was that good, I'd perk my ears right up to listen to what he had to say.

"Knowledgeable fella, ain't he?" Chance said as we made a stop that afternoon for water.

"He does appear to be that, son."

"I still don't trust him." Chance frowned. It was troubling him bad, as was evidenced by the look about him. "Something ain't right. The further I go with this buzzard, the more I just *know* something's not right."

"Seems to me your mind is still thinking like it was fighting that war you come back from, son," I said confidently. "You just ease up some. We're in good hands."

"I still don't like it," Chance said as he mounted up. My words hadn't soothed his worries at all.

After a moment of silence, he added, "I recall you getting that same kind of distrustfulness when we were tracking Comanches." He was about to say "way back when," but the words never came, stuck in his craw somehow. Still, it gave me a bit of hope to know that Chance was still able to call upon the memory of days long gone, especially since it was contrary to what he had proclaimed to me earlier. Maybe I hadn't lost these boys yet after all.

It was downright hot that afternoon, but it didn't bother me at all. No sir. I had some things of my own running through my mind when T.J. stopped talking and pointing here and there. I reckon that, just like Chance's comment the day before about me catching whatever was ailing T. J. Faro, I was beginning to catch Chance's own sickness, worrying. Mind you now, worrying is like one of those carnival rocking horses: *It'll keep you busy but you won't get a damn thing done.* If you know what I mean.

What I took to doing was pondering Chance's words and I'll be damned if the boy wasn't right. Somehow, things didn't seem quite right. Everything had been so easy out here so far. Except for the run-ins my boy was having with T. J. Faro, and those had been damn near every night we'd been on the trail. Thinking back on it, they almost seemed to take place right on time, right after supper. Almost as though they had been done to keep our minds off something else.

I spent the rest of that afternoon wondering if I had misjudged T. J. Faro; hell, if I'd misjudged my oldest boy and wasn't giving him enough credit for having the brains to think straight. After all, both of those boys had just come back from the war and both had survived, which takes a bit of doing if you think about it. Maybe I just hadn't been thinking about it.

One of the things that struck me as a mite out of place was how easily we had traveled the land. It wasn't until late in the afternoon that I'd remembered how Abel Ferris and I had fought back-to-back to settle the place we called Twin Rifles. For the most part, it was half the Comanche nation we had battled to get it done. If memory served me correctly, the Comanches hadn't acted civil toward a white man since the Council House Fight back in 1841. Yet we had been wandering through nearly two hundred miles of country in southwest Texas without so much as being noticed for over three days. It was realizing that which made me take Chance more seriously when he said what he did.

I rode up to the boys late that afternoon when we'd found a place that looked like a good camping spot. Neither one looked any too happy. Perhaps Chance's worries had been passed on to his little brother like some kind of bad cold.

"I been thinking about what you said, Chance," I said to the boy. "Thinking real hard on it all afternoon. You know, I think you're right."

"Then I say we do something about it," Chance said, bringing his hand down to his side and the newly holstered Colt's as he spoke.

"That would be a mistake, my friend," I heard T. J. Faro say from behind us. He had gone back to check something in his pack mule he had said. That put him behind Wash, Chance, and me. Chance glanced over his shoulder, his hand still firm on his revolver. I did the same and saw the same thing my boy did.

T. J. Faro had drawn both his Navy Colt's and had them trained on our backs. A chill ran down my spine, but worse was the embarrassing feeling inside me as I wondered how the hell I was going to explain this to my sons.

"Don't think of moving, my friends," Faro said

with a grin that continued to broaden. "For if I don't get you, they will." He motioned with his head toward the Pecos.

When the three of us looked back across the river, we saw what Faro was talking about. Out of nowhere, twelve well-armed men had appeared on horseback. Most of them were dressed much like T. J. Faro, in the style of the Mexican, wearing a sombrero and baubled vest with cotton shirt underneath. A handful of others wore no hat, instead sporting a bandana tied around their head. It crossed my mind that wearing only a bandana on your head wasn't too smart this time of year. Rifles, bowie knives, and pistols of one sort or another were not only on their person but strapped to their horses and saddles as well. They looked like a small army ready to go to war.

For my money, they were Comancheros.

CHAPTER

★ 15 ★

T. J. Faro waved an arm in the air, signaling the Comancheros across the river that it was safe to cross over. All the while his grin broadened and all the while I was working up an urge to pull my gun out and shoot him and be done with it, certain death or not.

"I hate being taken in, Faro," I growled in as hateful a voice as I'd conjured up in some time, even since the boys had come back. "You almost had me believing there was some good in you. Made me out to be a damn fool is all you did." I turned to my boys, who were watching the twelve mounted men cross the river. "Sorry I got you into this, boys. It's my fault," I said with regret. "I didn't mean for this to happen like it has."

Suddenly, a grin came to Chance's face, an unexplainable grin that I hadn't seen in a long time. "Pa,

Wash, I just remembered something. That riding we did as rangers before the war, you recall that?"

"Yeah." Wash smiled and I couldn't blame him. It was back then that he was trying his hardest to prove he was just as much a man as his brother or me. Those adventures had been pure fun for Wash, as I recalled.

"What about 'em?" You'd have to pardon me all to hell and gone if I wasn't laughing and singing about the predicament we'd gotten ourselves into, or days gone by.

"Seems to me that as much as we fought one another any other day of the week, when those times came around that we got stuck between a rock and a hard place, we shined best. Did a lot of working together to get it done too, ary my memory serves me right."

"Well, now, Chance, I'm glad as can be to see that your memory is as sharp as your tongue," I said with a tad bit of acid to my words. "But in case you hadn't noticed, son, these fellas are carrying what I would call one helluva arsenal. And they're about to take *our* guns to boot!"

"He's right, Chance," Wash confirmed. "Why, Kelly's Hardware Store ain't got *that* many firearms." The riders were getting closer now, making it more evident that we had miscounted the number of guns and other weapons these armed men carried. But that didn't seem to do much to Chance and that grin of his.

"That may be, brother, but the day ain't over yet." Then, in a more serious tone of voice, he added, "Neither is my life." These words from a man who said he wanted no more fighting.

He was headed for trouble, wanting it as badly as a wild horse daring to be broken, and not caring one way or another how you tried doing it. Fact of the matter is, I doubt that you could take the spirit from Chance unless you tried bleeding him, like some of those bronc busters over Louisiana way take a notion to every once in a while.

They were across the river now, approaching us with as much consternation as we must have been showing them. The difference was they got to looking a lot uglier a lot faster than we did. But then, this breed of plug uglies was born to that way of life. A scarred, dark-eyed hombre was leading the bunch, and it was he who made the mistake of mouthing off at Chance.

"Gringo," he said in a voice as ugly as his face. It wasn't the first time that me or my boys had been called a gringo by some fellow with a Spanish ancestry. I can understand that, I truly can. Brought my boys up to show a good deal of respect for another man's ancestry. Yes, I did. But old Plug Ugly here went one step too far when he spit on Chance's chest.

That tore it!

"Go to hell!" Chance growled and was off his saddle as soon as the words were out of his mouth. Truth to tell, he jumped into Plug Ugly as hard as he could, knocking the both of them off the Comanchero's horse so they rolled onto the ground and near the water washing ashore. Like I say, Chance is a feisty one and he got in some good licks in those first few seconds, bloodying the man's nose and mouth. But those few seconds were all he had, for another rider was soon at Plug Ugly's side. He brought the butt of his rifle down alongside Chance's head and my boy staggered only a step or two before falling unconscious. Plug Ugly commenced to pick up his rifle, fire in his eyes, but was stopped by T. J. Faro.

"Oh, no, amigo," he said, "don't you go a-killing

him yet. These are our *friends*. There'll be time for killing. You just let 'em stew a while. Let 'em think on how they're gonna die. I got something special in mind." He winked, nodded in final approval. "Besides, I got some more supplies here for us."

They let out a cheer, forgetting the near death incident that had just taken place. It was as though they were a bunch of small kids who don't have an attention span of more than five minutes or so. It was both amazing and curious, but it had saved our skins, so I wasn't about to question it. If nothing else, it was buying us time to figure out what to do next.

"He's gonna have one helluva lump on his head when he comes to, Pa," Wash said. He'd dismounted and quickly gone to his brother's side. Maybe there was something to what Chance had said about us working best when the odds were against us. It sure was showing up in Wash right quick. Come to think of it, every time Chance's life had been in danger, Wash had made a habit of stepping in to intervene in one way or another.

Wash had gained strength while he'd been away. The Comancheros were pulling our guns from our belts and saddle scabbards, but Wash paid little attention to them as he squatted down and hoisted his brother's big frame up on his shoulders and made his way to Chance's horse, draping him over the saddle.

We crossed the Pecos just a tad bit upstream, at a shallow place in the river. It couldn't have been more than knee-deep, which gave Chance's horse free movement without coming close to drowning his unconscious rider. I don't know what they could have been worried about, for the dozen of them rode around us like some boxed square all the way across the Pecos.

There were cottonwoods on the far side of the Pecos, down in a gully that served as a fine hiding place as well as a camp. Once off our horses, we were led to a tree and told to sit quietly while they bound our hands behind us and also tied our feet.

Chance didn't come to for a good fifteen minutes after we'd been tied up. His eyes came open briefly, then he squinted them tight and then much tighter, realizing the reason for the pain I knew he was feeling. Then he saw Wash and me, although it must have pained him to turn his head in either direction.

"Didn't know they had the iron horse this far west," he said.

"They don't," I said, a mite confused at first.

"Damn," he muttered. "I sure do feel like I've been run over by one of them beasts."

"Rifle butts do the same thing," Wash said. "I reckon having a hard head comes in handy at times, huh, Chance?"

"You see how you'd react to a sorry ass like that fool when he gobs a mouthful of tobacco juice on your chest. Smelling it is what brought me to," he said, then took a whiff of his chest and quickly turned away, making the kind of face I could only recognize from his youth, when he was sick and his mother forced medicine down his throat.

"What do you got in mind now, Pa?" Wash asked.

"I wouldn't discuss that until after sundown, amigos," T. J. Faro said with a grin, as he neared us. "My compadres, they wouldn't take kindly to it."

"I got a notion them compadres of yours don't take kindly to none but their own kind," Chance said, although it was hard telling whether it was his natural hard talking self coming through now, or the memory of why it was he got that bump on his head that put the gruffness in his voice. "That be a fair estimation, would it?"

Faro shrugged noncommittally. To me, he said, "This boy of yours, he's finally using his brain."

"Asked a fair question too, Faro," I said. "Asked a question that needs answering." I felt my own ire building a fire within me. Like I said, I don't like being taken in.

I struck a chord with that man that didn't make him feel comfortable, not at all. I reckon I'd reminded him that he was dealing with another man who considered himself a man of honor, and when you're dealing with that element, you'd better be straight as an arrow in your dealings. If you don't, you'll lose all respect the other man has for you. I was making T. J. Faro feel guilty, is what I was doing.

"Look, amigo," he said, a crusty frown building on his face as he squatted down in front of me, "I said I could lead you to those Comancheros who done in your woman, and that's all I said I would do." He struck his chest with a fist. "I didn't say I was gonna do your *fighting* for you, did I?

"Let me tell you something, Carston," he hissed, poking a finger into my chest as he spoke. "If you and your boys had tried to take on this bunch at the Pecos, they would have shot you out of your saddles! That's stupid!

"That's the difference between you and me, Carston," he said, the grin slowly coming back to his face. "You just lost your woman and you're thinking with your heart, not your head. And you know something? I watched you. You are stubborn enough to have pulled out those rifles and tried to take on these bandidos back at the Pecos. Without even taking cover! I got plans for how you're gonna die, Will

Carston. Oh, yes." His words had conjured up an evil look of madness in those beady little eyes of his as he spoke.

"I suppose you ain't got a family anymore," Chance said.

"No, my friend," T. J. Faro said, moving around the tree to Chance. "They been dead for years. My wife died giving birth to my boy, and the boy is gone now too." Out of the corner of my eye, I could see the madness building in him, reaching a peak like some volcano nearing eruption. Chance had the unfortunate circumstance of being in the man's presence when the volcano exploded.

"Then you came!" Faro shouted. "They were almost gone from within, but then you came!" Suddenly he lashed out and I heard the flat of his hand strike Chance across the face.

"You sonofa—" Chance started to say, but twice more T. J. Faro struck out, striking my boy hard with the flat of his hand, making a sound that could be heard throughout camp. In fact, we even had a couple of spectators now, although I doubt that they understood half the conversation or what it was about.

"You want to fight him, why don't you take him in a fair fight, mister?" Wash said, the mad building in him too. Like I say, he was getting right protective of his big brother of late.

"Fair?" Faro moved to Wash now. "Let me tell you something, *sonny*. It wasn't fair for you and your brother to come to Hell City, that's what wasn't fair. It wasn't fair for you to bring all the torment that you did, to make me remember what I've been trying to forget all these years. What would you know about fair, young one? You don't know nothing at all."

He spit on Wash and stomped off, mad as could be.

133

"He sure is a mean one, Pa," Wash said as he watched the man go.

Chance spit a mouthful of blood off to my side.

"Ain't that the goddamn truth."

Me, I had a notion that Faro was about to cry. Something was tearing him up inside and I thought I had an idea of what it was.

"I think there's more to him than either of you boys know," I said after a while.

"Aw, come on, Pa," Wash said defiantly. "Face it, he ain't nothing but a heartless old bastard."

"I think you're wrong," I said softly enough so only they would hear my words. "Between the three of us, I think we've opened up some old wounds he thought were healed. Trouble is those kind of wounds never do heal, not all the way."

"What are you talking about, Pa?" Chance asked in a voice filled with confusion.

"Believe it or not, I think old T. J. Faro sees his own son in the both of you. And I think that's bringing out a madness in him that he thought he'd overcome."

"You're talking in circles, Pa," Wash said.

"No, I'm not. I'm talking like a man who's felt the pain of another man and knows what it's like," I said.

"You're still not making sense," Wash said.

"All that question asking you done, Wash, was what reminded T.J. of his son in the boy's youth, got him to talking about all the things he never did do with him."

"But he spit on me!"

"This is a hard land, son. Times like this, there's no room for sentiment . . . or weakness. Men like T.J. hate weakness, and justifiably so. I've been in more than one fix where I felt that way."

"I suppose I'm his wayward son," Chance said, spitting out more blood.

"You ask me, you're the tough hombre his boy grew up to be. Remember, he said the boy went the wrong way in life."

"And he didn't like that in the boy, so he took to beating," Chance said, adding another clue.

"Likely. Ain't many a man didn't get a whipping from his daddy somewhere in his youth." I paused a moment to give my boys a chance to comment, but neither did. "I've got a notion that's part of what's bothering T.J. Beating him must have drove the boy away from his father.

"Those scars on his face and collar are a mite old. It took him a while to forget, I think. Maybe sitting behind that bar and listening to the troubles of others is what made him forget."

"I still don't see what you're getting at, Pa."

"T. J. Faro is real well versed in how he got that scar. But you know, boys, I don't think it's getting the scar that's kept his memory alive. No sir. I think the man who put it there was his son. I think his son left home and come back a badder man than T.J. wanted to see. I think he tried to do in his own father with a bowie knife. Boys, I think T. J. Faro killed his own son."

So much for that conversation. We sat there the rest of the afternoon in silence.

CHAPTER

★ 16 ★

I don't think a one of those yahoos would have fed us that evening if it hadn't been for T. J. Faro. Or maybe it was because he was one of only a few who were still sober at sundown. Most of his friends had taken to looking at the moon through the neck of a bottle or jug, and feeling right good about what they saw. Or maybe it was what they *thought* they saw. You take to drinking as much Who-Hit-John as these fellows were doing, and there was no telling what you'd be seeing, be it in your dreams or right smack dab in front of you.

"How come you ain't out there drinking with your friends?" Chance asked when Faro brought us three plates of frijoles and what looked to be Indian bread. From the crook in his arm dangled a strap with a canteen at the end of it.

"Do I look stupid?" Faro snorted. "I will serve you as much of that poison as you want, amigo, but don't ask me to drink it with you." He gave Chance a knowing look. "Why do you think I call it poison, eh?"

"Give me some water. I'm getting tired of tasting blood every time I swallow," Chance said.

T.J. nodded in silence, uncapped the canteen, and poured enough liquid into Chance's mouth so he could swish it around and spit out the blood, part of which was beginning to cake at the corner of his mouth. To my surprise—even more to Chance's I reckon—T.J. wiped the caked blood away and gave the boy a huge gulp he could swallow and really taste. Remember what I said about the weather getting hotter with each passing day? Well, hoss, even under those cottonwoods it got to be hotter than the devil unless there was a cooling breeze that came along, and I hadn't felt one all day.

"What excuse did you give these Comancheros for feeding us?" Wash asked. "Ain't you gonna look suspicious doing this?"

"At first I thought it would be hard, amigo," T.J. said, dishing food silently into Chance's mouth. "Then I told them that I wanted to be able to sleep good tonight and that if you were not fed properly, you would bellyache all night long." He chuckled to himself. "See, I got good at thinking too."

I was looking over my shoulder at Faro feeding Chance when I saw a distraught look cross his face. Following it was a sneer. "That's right, amigo," he said to Chance in a growl. "Eat good now, for tomorrow at sunrise you will die."

The words shocked Chance as much as they did Wash and me, I reckon, but it was Chance who had the food in his mouth. He half-swallowed the food, then spit it out, and then was choking on it. It was about then that T. J. Faro grabbed Chance by the back of the neck and pushed his head down between his legs, giving the boy a couple of good hard whacks on the back as he did.

"Terco, mi amigo," T.J. said as he worked over Chance. I looked back to my front and saw a man dressed in the Mexican way who must have been taller and heavier than either Faro or myself. His eyes were dark and shifty and his face a rugged one which, if looked upon in the right light, might have been considered handsome at one time. Unlike T. J. Faro, he was clean shaven and chose not to hide the cut that scarred the left side of his face. Such men have a way of looking upon this as being manly, but I had never thought of it as being so. He wore a well-kept mustache. For all his neatness he might have been the leader of this group of men, but I found that hard to believe since he held a bottle of whiskey in his hand, as did many of his henchmen. "I was just telling these hombres that they will meet their death tomorrow morning." Another chuckle as T.J. thumped Chance on the back again. "You can see they have little stomach for such things in life."

"They play the role of cowards, just as you said, Faro." Terco, or whatever his name was, had the deep resounding voice that fit his size and, more than likely, his character as well. But with nearly half of the bottle's contents gone, his voice had taken on a bit of a slur. It would take another bottle of whiskey to penetrate the man's full size, but at the rate he was drinking, I would lay odds that by midnight he would be dead to the world. Terco grinned at me in a lopsided way, turned and left.

"You're gonna have us shot at dawn, is that it?" Wash said, his ire coming alive. "Cowards, huh?"

Faro shrugged as he continued to feed Chance. "I had to tell them something."

Wash made up his mind to keep his mouth shut except for taking in food when T.J. fed him, once he was through with Chance. I had a notion the boy was mad at being used the way T. J. Faro was using him, both to ease his conscience and as bait in a trap. It was becoming more and more evident that T. J. Faro was in this for himself, and that meant that things didn't look very good for any of us Carstons at all. No sir.

I sat there thinking about Faro, wondering what made him tick. He was a difficult man to take apart in your mind, an even harder man to understand, yet, I found myself thinking that somewhere in the man was a shred of decency. How do you take a man who takes great pride in being called honorable on the one hand and then turns around and pulls his guns on you when your back is turned? It was hard to figure, but something told me that he was more than just tough. Something told me he had a lot of hurt in him that, because he was big and tough, he could never explain to anyone else for fear of losing that sense of manhood.

Or maybe I was looking at him differently than my sons did because I shared something with him that was very rare. It was something that haunted a man for the rest of his life once he'd done it, something that even on good days, lingered in the back of his mind and continually asked him why it had to happen. It could only happen to one in a million men, but it had happened to T. J. Faro and me. We had each killed one of our own flesh and blood.

Wife or son, it didn't matter. In the end we could

139

both of us justify what we'd done. Cora had been stark raving mad and had begged me to kill her, to put her out of her misery. Although I couldn't prove it and would never ask, I had a notion that T. J. Faro's boy had been begging to be done in too when he'd come back after his father. But like I said, I couldn't prove any of it.

"You understand, of course, I've got to feed you like this," Faro said, when he got around to me. "Ary I cut you fellers loose, why they'd figure I was feeding you on your honor, or some foolish thing like that."

I nodded that I understood as I chewed my beans and bread.

"One thing I'll say," Chance commented. "Only thing good that's come out of the day so far has been the food. Union food wasn't all that good."

"What they fed us in the Confederacy was worse, and sometimes nonexistent," Wash said. "Corn bread wasn't half bad though."

T. J. Faro had a look about him as he shoveled the food down my gullet, a look that said he was getting nervous about something. He got me curious and I found myself chewing and swallowing faster.

"All right, Faro," I said when I was through and had taken a couple of good pulls on what remained of the canteen water. "I ate it up, now you spit it out. I want to hear what it is you got to say, and I know it's something."

T.J. licked his lips hard, although I doubt that there was any wetness to them when he did.

"All right, Carston, you asked for it," he said, committing himself to the truth. Those shifty eyes moved about more suspiciously than usual now, making sure I was the only one who would hear his words. "You saw the one I called Terco, the tough one. No

140

one knows his real name, nor will they ask. He's one of the lieutenants here. Fancies himself some kind of lady's man." As the words came out, I could feel a deep dark furrow forming on my forehead, for I knew only too well what it was he would wind up saying, but I let him speak the words. I had to hear it for myself. "Half of what I had packed in that mule of mine was bottles of whiskey that hadn't quite fermented yet. Hell, these buzzards are so hard drinking they'll drink straight grain alcohol, which is what most of this stuff is, with a touch of chewing tobacco added for color.

"Well, I ain't seen a good share of these fellas in close to a decade now, so we had a lot of catching up to do. Terco, he's been around that long too. Keeps going by instilling fear in those around him, I reckon. Well, he's bragging about all these conquests he's had and keeps on about one wild cat he had not long ago. Kicked and screamed and yelled something fierce, he says she did. Had to knock her out a couple of times before he took her.

"The way he talked about how feisty she was and what he done got me a mite more suspicious. So I asks him whereabouts this place be and he tells me." T. J. Faro sniffled some and looked aside as he ran a sleeve across his nose.

"And?" If I said it hard and demanding, it was because I meant it that way, although I doubt I could have helped say it any other way.

"I'd say it was Terco and some of his lads who hit your ranch and done in your woman, Will. No two ways about it, son, you hit the jackpot."

CHAPTER

★ 17 ★

When the sun fell away from the face of the earth that afternoon I couldn't tell you. Me, I was consumed in a building hatred that I was certain was going to see me dead before the next day was out. All I recall was that when I noticed it next, the sun had disappeared as though some blanket had been thrown over us, blocking out the light. If it wasn't for the moon, which wasn't quite full, it would have been pitch-black out. There were good points and bad about the fullness of the way the moon set that night, but I didn't confront those until later on. At the moment I was mad enough to put a choke hold on anyone who got on the wrong side of me, especially a Comanchero by the name of Terco.

"Look like you're ready to bust a vein, Pa," Chance said about an hour into the night. I muttered something, only half-hearing him, for I was in another world of my own.

Call it grief if you like, or memories of times gone by, take your pick. All I could think about was the life I'd shared with Cora and how much she had meant to me all of those years we'd been together. It was me and Abel Ferris who had fought to make what was once a camp site into the likes of a town and damn near lost our lives doing it. That was over thirty years ago. Now Cora was gone and so was Abel. At the moment all I could think, all I could feel, was how much I missed Cora and how I wanted her by my side. But I didn't feel ready to leave this mortal earth to do it, you understand. The survivor in me was telling the common sense part of my brain that we had to get out of here, and that was making me mad.

If waiting is what drives a man to near insanity while the tension of battle—or a coming death— rises, then it is mad that keeps him going once that fever pitch is aroused in him. Me, I was nearing that fever pitch, knowing in me that I could bust loose of these ropes any minute now, I was getting that mad.

But I didn't have to waste my strength on busting loose from those ties. About two hours into the night, T. J. Faro came slowly waddling over to our tree once again. A little breeze had come across the Pecos, picking up the coolness of the water with it, giving relief from the sweltering heat of the day. Faro had donned a buckskin jacket, open at the waist, folded blankets draped over one arm in front of him. Even with the loose fit of the buckskin jacket, he looked as though he had gained some weight.

"You're getting to be a right frequent visitor for a man who turned us over to these vultures," Chance said with a frown.

"You want blankets for the night, amigo," T. J. Faro said in a testy way. All of a sudden he was acting like a man who wanted in the worst way to perform a good deed and was having one hell of a time doing it. He kept looking over his shoulder suspiciously, but he needn't have worried for the camp had grown silent within the past hour, most of its occupants passed out like the stinking drunks they were, empty whiskey bottles lying near them where they had fallen into unconsciousness. "There's only one guard out there, but I've got to be careful about this, for there's no telling where Chico is," he said as he squatted down beside me.

"What's going on?" I asked, again confused by the man's actions and words.

"When I get through here, Will Carston, you can't say that I never did nothing for you except give you a hard time or watered-down whiskey." Stripping one of the blankets from his arm, he unfolded it and spread it lengthwise over my legs, pausing at my feet as he looked carefully about camp again. "Whatever I do here now, Will, *don't move,* comprende?"

"If you say so." I was beginning to have a good feeling about T. J. Faro again, my faith suddenly restored in the man I had once called honorable. Eyes still darting about, his hands moved in a natural manner as a bowie knife appeared in one hand and he cut the bonds that tied my feet. Suddenly, he was moving about like a scared rabbit, cutting loose the ropes that tied my wrists. But I didn't move, much as I wanted to. Instead I rubbed my wrists and did what I could to get the circulation flowing in my hands once more. The real surprise came when T.J. placed my Remington .44 beneath the blanket on my lap. It was then I knew for sure that I hadn't misjudged him.

144

"Don't feel foolish, Will Carston," he said. "I told you I'd do something and I say what I mean and mean what I say, just like you taught your boys. I've just got a strange way of doing things, that's all. I have my own code of honor."

"Never doubted it for a minute," I said, finding myself now speaking in the same soft tones as T.J.

He moved around to my rear, between Chance and Wash, and began to work feverishly on them in the same way he had me. But his silence was short-lived, for he had something to say to them too.

"It is you two who are the real *fools* here," he said to both of my boys.

"Cut me loose and I'll show you what kind of fool I am," Chance challenged the man.

"Shut up, Chance," I said in as low a voice as I could. "The man's doing us a favor." The boy must have heard me or else T.J. was undoing his ties and arming him the same as he had me and Chance was getting to see what I meant, for his voice was at once still.

"You two are the fools." T.J. snorted. "I see the look about you. I can tell. You still fight the war. And you are like all of the others who do the same. You all fight about *who* is right when the real question is always *what* is right. Fools," I heard him mutter. My boys couldn't think of anything to mouth off about at T.J.'s words, for they got awful quiet then.

"You must stay here until I tell you it is time," T.J. said when he was through freeing our bonds and arming all three of us.

"Why not now?" Chance asked in a whisper.

"I have yet to take care of your horses, amigo. When you leave, you will have all of your rifles and pistols, as well as your mounts. You may need them on your

145

journey back to your town. The mule will be of no use to you, for there are no more supplies." He chuckled as he glanced over his shoulder at the dimming fire and the drunken Comancheros lying about it. "My compadres have drunk all of them."

"What about you?" Wash asked.

T. J. Faro shrugged. "I can take care of myself. I know this type. They lie to one another all the time. I will be no different in stretching the truth, and thus, no worse off than they are. But first I must ready the horses."

"T.J.?"

"Yes."

"Thanks."

"Por nada, amigo." Then he was gone.

I do believe that was about the slowest hour of my lifetime that passed by next. I didn't know where Terco was but I was determined to find him before we left this camp and kill him just as dead as my Cora had wound up. It was the one thing I had gone on this mission for, and I would not be denied the pleasure of killing the man responsible for my wife's death. No matter what T.J. had in mind, killing this bastard was my sole reason for living right now.

"If our horses are still over in the clearing, boys," I said in a whisper as we waited for T.J.'s signal, "you hightail it over to 'em and get the hell out of here. I'll be along directly."

"Not without you, Pa," Wash said.

"T.J. was right. You're fools. Won't even listen to your own father."

"You ain't the only one wants to see this Terco fella dead, Pa," Chance said. In a way it made sense, for I'd forgotten that Cora had been their mother as well as my wife. Besides, Chance and Wash had come a long ways with me on this ride, a long ways in more ways than one, I was thinking, so they had a right to see Terco die just as much as I did, I reasoned.

It was an hour before T.J. returned, still carefully darting his beady eyes about camp.

"Chico is the only one to worry about now. He is over by the horses. But I will take care of him," he said. "Terco is in the far corner over there," he added, pointing across the camp. "When you take care of him, do it slowly, for you will wake the camp. I must tell you, amigo, that even in a drunken stupor, some of these bandidos are fast with a gun. Your horses are ready."

Then he was gone, moving as fast as a scared rabbit over to the entrance to the clearing.

A silent nod between us was all that was needed to set things in motion. Ever so softly we pulled back the blankets and got to our feet, each of us with a six-gun in hand. I spotted the big mass of a man who must be Terco, the man T.J. had pointed out who was as dead to the world as the rest of his friends. I bypassed the fire by instinct, but truth to tell, I could have walked right through it and wouldn't have noticed the difference, my thinking was centered on killing Terco that much. When we reached him, Chance stood on his right side, I on his left, and Wash at his feet.

"Time to open the ball," Wash said and gave the man a swift kick in the feet with his well-heeled boot. The shock jolted Terco awake, but I reckon if that didn't wake him, the sight of three gringos standing over him, armed with a pistol each, must have sobered him up right quick.

Chance leaned over the man, grabbing the Mexican's belt knife as he spoke. "I'd give every life I took in the war to be there when you came and raped my ma, you sonofabitch. But this is as good as I'll get." In a movement that was lightning quick, Chance slashed the man's throat with his own knife before dropping it on the ground at his side.

Blood began to spurt from his throat as he tried in vain to yell a warning to the camp and save his own life at once.

"You sorry bastard," I mumbled through the tears as I cocked my Remington. "If you ain't the most miserable sonofabitch to come into my life—" I wanted to continue but couldn't. The urge to kill the man outweighed the need for him to know why he was dying. I stretched my arm out in front of me, as though placing the gun closer to his head would make him any deader when I pulled the trigger. If it satisfied some death wish then I reckon I got through it, for when I pulled the trigger the bullet went through the middle of his skull and lifted his head from the ground as the bullet smashed out the other side. The sorry son of a bitch who called himself Terco, the tough one, had died hearing his own screams caught in his throat and what was left of his mind.

I turned to go but not before I saw Wash place a bullet in the man's elsewheres. As grotesque as it seemed, I wasn't about to hold a conversation with my boy about the why and wherefore of what he had done. I would never talk to either of my boys about what we had done today, not even if we lived through the day. From the movement around us, I was getting the feeling that this was going to be our day to die as well.

T.J. was right about some of these yahoos having good reflexes even when they were half drunk. We were making our way back across the camp to the clearing where the horses were waiting for us when

148

two of the Comancheros scattered about the ground came to, guns in hand. Surprise must have gone through their minds as they began to put their guns to use, but beginning to was as far as they got. Chance killed one where he lay and Wash killed the other. Oddly enough, it crossed my mind that they weren't bad shots for being on the run. Then I remembered that we were Texas Rangers and we were required to be able to shoot like that. Suddenly, I had a fierce pride in myself and my boys, the same pride I'd once felt so long ago when all three of us were rangers and there hadn't been a war to tear us apart. I had a distinct knowledge once again of the power of the gun and the power to take a life it gave a man.

The camp was coming awake now, gun smoke filling the air as those coming out of a drunken stupor searched around for their handguns. I had a notion that T.J. had strategically misplaced them in the case of each of the Comancheros, which added a few more seconds to our escape from this camp.

I must have looked strange, trying to run across that clearing with that hitch in my git along, but I did the best I could, even though my boys had reached the clearing in no time flat. They always had been good at footraces.

"Chico! Chico!" I heard T.J. yell at the clearing. "They are getting away!" At first I thought I'd been tricked again by T. J. Faro, for it was getting to be a ritual with the man to do things out of the ordinary, or at least without explaining himself to us. But it turned out I was wrong.

The man called Chico was a short squat man of Mexican ancestry. He must have been out by the horses, for he came running from that direction as he entered the clearing. T.J. didn't appear to have any weapon with him, so the man was going to go to the aid of his friends by running right past T.J. Me and my boys stayed off to the side and out of the way as much as possible as the Mexican ran past T.J.

The trouble was, he never made it past T. J. Faro. Our friend stuck his foot out, tripping the man as his own weight took him to the ground face first, jarring the Henry rifle from his grip as it clattered to the ground. Wash stepped out in the open to pick it up, an action that brought Chico to his knees, but no further than that. With a viciousness I had never seen in the man before, T. J. Faro took one step behind the man and dug Chance's bowie knife into the small of his back. Chico's body went limp and he groaned as T.J. twisted the bl de around inside the boy, making him die that much quicker and that much more painfully. Then, as cool as a cucumber, T.J. yanked out the bowie knife, wiped the blood on Chico's jacket, and handed Chance the knife.

"You got a good sharp knife, amigo," he said with a smile.

"Thanks," Chance said, taking the knife. He thrust it in its scabbard at his side. Then, miracle of miracles, he smiled at T.J. as though the two men were genuine friends and had been all along.

"Vaya con Dios, amigo," T.J. said with a smile that had a good bit of warmth to it. I had a notion he was experiencing the same feeling I was.

"Sure," Chance said. You would have thought that in those few seconds they had a total understanding of one another. But it didn't last that long.

I saw Chance suddenly frown as he looked at T.J. Then I realized he wasn't looking *at* T.J., he was looking *past* him.

Chance had swung a hard right at T.J. and knocked him ass over teakettle, but it wasn't because of some hatred he felt. By the time my boy had done that, I saw what he had seen first. Two more Comancheros were coming across the camp, half-pulling up their pants and half-running.

Chance looked at them, then looked down at the astonished look on T. J. Faro's face, and snapped off a shot at T.J. that landed next to his hand.

"There, amigo," Chance said. "I saved your life."

In the meantime, Wash had stepped in beside his brother and put one slug from the Henry rifle into one of the charging men's guts, then peppered three or four more at the second man's feet, making him do an Irish jig before losing his balance and falling down.

As T.J. had promised, our horses were ready to ride. That was just what we did too—ride the hell out of there. I noticed that he took one more precaution and gave us a bit of a head start by hobbling the rest of the Comancheros' horses.

To say we rode like the wind would be putting it mildly. We rode south along the Pecos like there wasn't a tomorrow. There would be plenty of time to cross to the other side once we were far enough away. At the moment we had to get far enough away.

I had all sorts of things rushing through my mind as we dug our heels into our mounts for about half an hour. I don't know what kind of ground we covered, but it was considerable. Never did see anyone coming after us either. In an odd sort of way that was strange. Or maybe it wasn't. This was the first time I'd had anything to do with Comancheros, and perhaps they had a reputation spread far and wide enough so that they didn't care whether we got away or not. That started me to thinking and when I got to thinking, I pulled in the reins of my horse and led him over to the Pecos for water.

"What're you stopping for, Pa?" Wash asked.

"I just got to thinking, boys," I said, scooping up a handful of water after dismounting. It's surprising how out of breath a body can get just riding a horse, when it's the horse who does all the work. Purely amazing.

"What about, Pa?" Chance began to rustle through his saddlebags, searching for something.

"That I recall, those Comancheros burning our place to the ground was the first time we've ever had any truck with them around Twin Rifles. Mind you, now, I had to fight off plenty of Comanches when we settled that place, but not a one of them Comancheros. No sir."

"What're you driving at?" Wash always was the curious one.

"Well, G.W., it's like this. You find rats bothering you and yours, why, you naturally want to get rid of 'em and discourage the rest of 'em from coming back."

"True."

"So you get rid of 'em by laying out a good thick dose of poison and killing 'em all off."

"Sure. But I still don't follow you."

"Well, son," I said, "it seems to me that these Comancheros are a lot like rats that prey on the general population. They pretty well know where we come from, because T.J. said that Terco fella had a big mouth. I'm thinking some of those yahoos with him back there were likely with him when he raided our ranch house."

"I see," Wash nodded. "And you're wanting to issue a mite of lead poisoning to thin these fellows out?"

"Not really," I said, stroking my jawline in thought. "What I've got in mind is more on the line of extermination. That way I won't have to look over my shoulder and wonder when Twin Rifles is gonna get another Comanchero raid."

"No need to ask, Pa." Wash nodded in affirmation. "I'm with you. Just let me check the loads in this Henry and we can be on our way." Then he looked at Chance, who was still going through his saddlebags. "What about you, Chance?"

"Huh?" Then his older brother muttered, "Damn," in that frustrated way he had. "What was that?" he said, looking up.

"Pa and me are going back to that Comanchero camp. Gonna teach those fellas the meaning of life. You in?"

"Hell, yes," Chance said with a good deal of enthusiasm. "Hell, yes, I'll go."

Once again that pride swelled up in me, remembering the brief scene between T. J. Faro and Chance as we had left.

"Going back to give T.J. a hand, are you, son?" I asked proudly.

"Hell, no." He frowned. Then, looking down at the gun belt that had been taken away from him and which he had gotten back, he added, "One of them sonsabitches has got my brand-new holster."

CHAPTER

★ 18 ★

I spent the better part of my youth up in the Shinin'
Mountains, trapping fur with the likes of Jed Smith,
"Broken Hand" Tom Fitzpatrick, and the Sublettes. I
also managed to get a decent education in an institute
we called the Rocky Mountain College, where we'd sit
around during those months of the winter that were
colder than the devil and read and discuss books that
certain members of the group had the foresight to
bring along for just such occasions. We read Clark's
Commentaries on the Bible, various geology and
science books, even that Shakespeare fellow, who used
those powerful words. Or maybe it was just the way he
wrote them that was powerful. I remember he had a
quote in one of those plays about discretion being the
better part of valor. Well, hoss, we had our own
definition of such thoughts out here. Instead of quot-

ing Shakespeare, like some fancy easterner would, most folks out here just said that "sometimes it's better to pull your freight than to pull your gun."

I got to thinking about that as we rode on back toward the Comanchero camp. No man on earth would have condemned us for getting the hell out of that place the way we did. No sir. Fact of the matter was, going back like we were, why, I'd begun to wonder if we weren't all as mad as some of those kings that Shakespeare fellow was always spouting off about. Those fellows always did seem a mite round the bend, if you know what I mean. On the other hand, I was beginning to understand part of their reasoning now too. Hell, I was beginning to think I could understand that touch of madness I'd seen in T. J. Faro's eyes that one time too! Maybe we were all loony as a bird.

Whatever we were, we were all mad for one reason or another. Chance was mad about one of those yahoos taking his brand-new, handmade holster. Wash wasn't saying, but I had a notion he had developed a good deal of respect for T. J. Faro and the way he operated, putting his life on the line for us the way he did. Me, well, hoss, I reckon I'd gotten my revenge for Cora, but I didn't want these pilgrims swooping down on Twin Rifles like some buzzard looking for prey. I didn't want them injuring or killing more innocent people. I may not have had my badge on or been the official law, but keeping the peace was still my job in that town, and I had a definite yearning to get back to it now. There was just this one minor detail that had to be taken care of first, a certain amount of rats that needed to be taught a lesson.

We had the moon working for us that night, for like I say, it was near full and gave us the light to see where we were going, and I don't mind telling you that I was grateful for that. We rode back at an easy pace, expecting to be met by a mad bunch of Comancheros riding hell for leather in our direction. It's times like this that I remember that I ain't the only fellow on God's green earth who has the capacity for getting mad. Remembering that sort of thing tends to make you recall how mortal you really are, along with the cold, hard fact that you won't live forever.

About half the way back, we dismounted and walked our horses the rest of the way, having watched our back trail on our ride out and knowing what to look for. Besides, if they saw our outline in the night, we'd make perfect targets for them to practice shooting at. On the other hand, they shouldn't be looking for us, figuring us for the cowardly gringos T. J. Faro had told them we were.

"Why'd you shoot at T.J.'s hand after you knocked him down, Chance?" Wash said. Like I said, he always was the curious one.

"A handful of those fellas were starting to come at us and I didn't want them to get the idea that T.J. was helping us, so I hit him hard and then shot in the dirt like he had something in his hand. At least they wouldn't think he was on our side."

"Makes sense," I said in agreement. Chance might be giving his holster as the excuse for going back, but I was forming the notion that he was going back for T. J. Faro's sake as well. He just wasn't talking about it.

We spent the rest of the night walking those horses in silence, keeping an eye out for movement to our front. It was an hour before sunup when we reached the camp, but the night was still silent in the air. Had they gone back to sleep? Had they been drinking more whiskey after we left? Were they passed out again? In a way I was hoping so, for it would make getting rid of this type of vermin a lot easier. Of course, there was also the challenge of shooting a man face-to-face and surviving the ordeal. We had killed off at least three, and maybe four of the Comancheros upon leaving camp the first time, so that cut the odds against us to a tad less than three-to-one. If T. J. Faro could lend a hand, those odds would be cut to two-to-one, and most men could learn to handle those kinds of odds on a daily basis in a land like this. Who knew, we might survive this fight after all.

We stopped about fifty yards from camp and checked the loads on our guns again. Chance pulled his second pistol from his saddlebags and placed the caps in proper position. I did the same with a second Remington I had tucked away in my saddlebags. Wash only had that Dance Brothers revolver of his, but still carried the Henry he'd taken from Chico. I also knew he had that Colt's Revolving Rifle in his rifle scabbard.

"You ready?" I asked in a whisper.

"Not quite," Chance said. Then, fishing a hand around in his pocket, he pulled out his Texas Ranger badge and pinned it prominently on his shirt pocket.

"Do tell," I said, for it surprised me.

"These sonsabitches need to know there ain't no *cowards* in the group that's gonna do 'em in," he said in a testy tone. With a nod of his head, he added, "Damn bastards are gonna know it was Texas Rangers that killed 'em, by God!" He had acquired what I could only describe as a killing mean attitude, which meant I wouldn't have to look after this boy of mine any longer. No sir, he had come of age and could take care of himself, thank you kindly, sir.

"He's got my vote," Wash said and held out his own

157

Texas Ranger badge. "They might as well know it's the law that's come to clean house."

I couldn't believe my eyes. Just as though it were way back when and they were being called on to perform as rangers, they'd produced their badges without a second thought. Could they have tucked them away in their belongings when they'd gone off to war so long ago? I'd never thought to look. Nor had I thought to ask if they had the badges with them when we'd lit out after the Comancheros. But there they were as plain as day, so they must have toted the badges all through the war. Suddenly, I felt about these two men in a way I hadn't in a long time. What they had just done was saying a lot about the way they really felt about the rangers, whether they'd admit it or not. Hell, it said a lot about the way they felt about me too! Damn, but I was proud of them. "Never did leave home, did you?" I muttered under my breath.

"What was that, Pa?" Chance said, looking up from pinning on his badge.

"You boys trying to embarrass me, are you?" I said. I had carried my marshal's badge pinned inside my shirt ever since leaving Twin Rifles, but this seemed about the right time to let the law take a hand in this affair. Oh, it was revenge killing that we were doing, no doubt about it, but I reckon it feels better, or is done easier, if there's a badge on your chest to back you up, and I said as much to the boys.

"Hell," Chance said in a loud whisper, "seems to me it was years ago that you told us as long as you were right, you could nail 'em to the wall, no matter how many or who they were. You made a big fuss about this *particular* badge when you said it too, as I recall," he added, thumbing the badge on his chest.

He was right. I'd near forgotten those words so long

158

ago. But then, I reckon I'd forgotten a lot from long ago. Suddenly, I felt more pride rush through me, not for being a father so much as for being a ranger, a Texas Ranger. "A Texas Ranger can ride like a Mexican, trail like an Indian, shoot like a Tennessean, and fight like the very devil!" Rip Ford had first said those words back in '46 when we'd gone off to war against Mexico, and there wasn't a ranger alive who couldn't repeat it to you word for word. Chance had struck a chord in me. Maybe I was getting a mite old for not remembering it, but I was well aware of it now. Still . . .

"I do believe you've got a point there, son," I said quietly. "Once a ranger, always a ranger."

There wasn't anything left to say. Besides, it was time for doing now. When we neared the camp, we split up, Wash moving around to the north side, Chance circling the camp to the east side, and me coming in by the same entrance we had made our exit from. We were all playing it by ear, so I couldn't tell who would be the first into camp. Hell, I didn't really care, so long as we got rid of those pilgrims.

A new guard had replaced Chico next to the horses. He wasn't too attentive to what went on in the world around him. In fact, from a distance he looked awful blurry eyed. All of that grain alcohol must have taken its toll on those fellows. I'd bet a dollar they were all wanting a taste of the hair of the dog that bit them. I snuck up behind this fellow and laid the sharp end of the butt of my Remington up alongside his temple. The blow put him out of this world and he sank to the ground. I caught his rifle before he dropped it. Then I grabbed the back of his head and the front of his chin and snapped his neck, making sure he was on his way to meet his Maker.

T. J. Faro wasn't going to be an awful lot of good to us, if what I saw was any indication. No sir. Somehow, his friends didn't believe he hadn't had a part to play in our escape, for they now had him tied up and setting before the same cottonwood tree we had been sitting against.

"Come on, Faro," one of the Comancheros kneeling before him growled, "admit it! You helped the gringos escape. Admit it!"

T.J. had already been beaten, his left eye a swollen purplish mass, blood caking near the corner of his mouth. But he was a tough one all right. He still had the courage, or stupidity, depending on which side of the fence you were on, to spit a gob of blood into the man's face. The Comanchero's face filled with rage and he backhanded T.J., whose head snapped to the side as he groaned, only half-conscious. His hands were tied together in front of him and I had a sneaking suspicion that he had started out in a standing position, only to slump against the tree as his attackers beat him. A second man, a guard with a rifle at port arms, stood on the opposite side of T.J. The man kicked Faro in the side and I thought I saw the crotch of T.J.'s pants become suddenly wet from his urine.

And they were calling us cowards, I thought to myself. Chance was seeing the same thing I was and must have decided it was time to start the ball. Suddenly, he burst out in the open, a Colt's Army Model in each hand. The look in his eye was a crazy one that said he was here to do business.

"Fill your hands, you sonsabitches!" Chance all but yelled, as though he wanted the entire camp to take him on. "The rangers come to collect!" And collect he did! As though only one shot were fired, he pulled the triggers on those Colt's at the same time, placing a slug in the heart of each of the Comancheros at T.J.'s side. I thought I saw a spark of life return to T.J.'s eyes now, accompanied perhaps by the same pride I was feeling in my boy.

They were coming out of the wooded area now. I shot and killed a Comanchero coming out in the open at Chance's side, while he did the same to cover me. The odds were getting better all the time.

I heard Wash's gun go off to the north side of camp, then saw him step out in the open, looking for a target, a Comanchero dead at his feet.

"Stop or I'll kill him!" came a loud authoritative voice from Wash's way. Neither Chance nor I knew what was going on until the big man moved up behind Wash and in one quick motion knocked his revolver and rifle from his hands, placed a big arm around Wash's throat, and stuck his own pistol up to the boy's temple.

Chance and I gave each other a fast glance, for we had to make a decision now. Wash's life hung in the balance. I wanted these varmints gone and done with and I knew that Chance wanted the same. But I didn't think either one of us was willing to live with the kind of guilt that came with losing a son or a brother.

The gunfire had stopped now, the rest of these birds apparently thinking we were going to give in to them and hand over our firearms. The fact of the matter was that everyone had a gun in his hand now, ready to dish out instant death. I didn't know about Chance, but the palms of my hands were all of a sudden getting real sweaty. As it turned out, we didn't have to make that decision after all. T. J. Faro made it for us.

"No!" he yelled. *"Don't do it!"* By the time Chance and I could see what he had in mind, he had already fired the six-gun in his hand. All I could figure was that

161

he had gotten it from one of the dead men who had fallen next to him. However he came by it didn't seem to matter, for he used it well, firing only once and placing that one shot in the eye of the big man who was trying to use my son for a leverage point. The man's head jerked back and Wash fell to the ground on top of him, breaking his fall as the man fell under him.

Wash rolled to his side and grabbed his Henry rifle, eyeing one of the Comancheros who quickly disappeared into the trees.

At the same time another Comanchero, two guns in hand, fired away at T.J., hitting him twice in the chest, before turning his guns on Chance and firing twice again. I saw Chance jerk back and grimace, but he was a man with a mission and he would not be stopped. His own two guns fired again, hitting their mark and the man fell back.

Chance was standing there bleeding, looking for more targets as the gun smoke settled. Out of the corner of my eye I saw the man he had just shot cocking his six-gun with his last breath. I snapped a shot at his head and killed him, making sure that was the last thing he did on this earth.

"Sorry ass," I heard myself say as he died.

"Where's Wash?" Chance said, a note of concern in his voice. I told myself in that one split second that I was glad to hear that in Chance's voice. Maybe we'd all come a long way since we'd left Twin Rifles.

Then a shot rang out beyond the trees. I stepped out in the open more so I could see what was happening, then saw Wash standing there, smoke twirling up from the Henry in his hand, a riderless horse heading toward the horizon. It was the first time that morning that I'd taken note that the sun was rising.

"I think he just made buzzard bait out of the last of these yahoos," I said.

Taking a quick survey of the camp, Chance saw the same thing I did, massive death and not a bit of it going anywhere but straight to hell. The only one who still had a tad of life in him was T. J. Faro, but I think we all knew he wasn't long for this world.

Chance was looking about as peaked as T.J. when he nearly fell over trying to kneel beside the dying man.

"Damn it," Chance muttered, "here I go and save your life and you wind up looking like a sieve." Chance was about to pass out or cry, one, I couldn't be sure which. He'd taken a bullet high in his chest and was bleeding nearly as much as the man he was talking to. It just hadn't caught up with him yet. But then, that's usually the way it is when you haven't seen your own blood flowing out of you like it was from both of these two men.

It pained him to do it, but T. J. Faro smiled as he dropped his gun and placed a hand on Chance's knee.

"You got nerve, Chance," he said, "a lot of nerve."

"No," Chance said, "just a couple of guns."

"But it took nerve to come in here like you did, boy. You gotta know that."

"Mister Faro," Wash said, running up to us, "you're getting awful good at saving lives. I don't know how you fired that shot but I'm grateful to you."

"It's something else I got good at, kid." He was starting to fade now and I could tell it. I was kneeling down on his left side when he spoke his final words. "Will, give me a decent burial. An honorable man ought to have one."

"Sure, T.J.," I said, but by then I was talking to a dead man. T. J. Faro's head rolled to the side and his hand fell into my lap. Truth to tell, I didn't mind the blood that got all over my trousers.

Chance muttered something to himself. Then he squinted his eyes hard, opened them wide once to see what it was he had spied, and nodded his head.

"See," he said, "told you one of them sonsabitches had my holster." He began to reach for his brand-new, handmade holster but lost his balance and passed out on top of the guard he had only minutes before shot to death.

CHAPTER

★ 19 ★

We stayed at the camp for three days. I had a devil of a time getting that slug out of Chance after T.J. died and the fighting was over. When I was through, Wash and I determined that giving Chance a few days to get back his strength would be the best thing to do. Besides, these fellows had a fair amount of medicinals that they wouldn't be needing, so we made the most of them.

There was another reason we stayed, but I didn't tell Chance about it until the third day. Just like he requested, Wash and I dug a decent grave for T. J. Faro, one deep enough so the wolves and buzzards wouldn't get to him like they did the more shallow ones. I spent that first night working on a piece of wood for T.J.'s grave marker. We buried him the

165

second day. His tombstone had his name and the date of death, with these words:

HE DIED AN HONORABLE MAN

I couldn't do much better for T.J., but somehow I didn't figure he'd want much more.

We spent the second day dragging the bodies of the dead Comancheros to a position outside camp that was as downwind as you could get. We laid the bodies out, piling some on top of others and found as many rocks as we could to cover them. I spent that second night working on a piece of wood too. If any more Comancheros came around, I wanted them to get the idea that their friends here didn't fare so well and that it would do them well to watch where they went from now on.

The morning of the third day I placed that piece of hardwood at about the center of where the bodies were. We didn't say any kind words over them, for there were none. If anything, Wash and I spit with contempt on those partial graves. Their tombstone read:

THEY DREW FIVE ACES

"Now, what's that mean?" Wash asked.

"Well, son, they remind me a mite of T.J. in a way." I scratched my head, searching for the right words. "There was a gambler I run across back in the rush of '49. Got about as good at his cards as T.J., I reckon. Made a lot of money too. Trouble was one night he'd won so much money that he got excited about it and made the mistake of dealing himself four more aces!"

"Four more?"

166

"Hell, boy, he already had one!"

"What'd they do to him?"

"Why, they took him out and hung him, of course. Put them same words on his tombstone. Believe me, they said it all."

"Do you think whoever else sees this tombstone is gonna know what you mean?" he asked.

"They're gonna know these bastards overplayed their hand, just like that gambler, by trying to cheat the wrong men in the wrong game." I winked at Wash and he smiled, knowing that I meant the Carstons by the "men" I spoke of. Yes sir, we had come a long way since leaving Twin Rifles.

"What have you two been doing?" Chance asked on the third day. He'd spent most of the previous two days unconscious and sweating like the devil. The best we could do for him once I'd gotten the bullet out was fill him up with water as often as we could and pray the Maker wasn't looking for any more occupants for that place he called Heaven.

"Digging," Wash said.

Chance frowned in confusion before a worried look crossed his face. He sat up on one elbow, took a fast look about him, squinted, and said, "Where's T.J.? Where's the rest of 'em?"

"Out yonder," I said, tossing a thumb over my shoulder. "You lie still, boy. Wash, get your brother some of them frijoles and Injun bread he liked so well."

"Throw in some coffee and you've got a deal," Chance said. He lay back down, gathering his thoughts for a minute while Wash rustled up some grub for him. With a grin, he said, "I sure hope Rachel can remember how to panfry a steak."

"Son, you get back alive and tell her what you've

been through and I guarantee you she'll cook for you for free for the rest of your life."

Chance chuckled, then coughed. When it passed he chuckled some more.

"You don't know how long I've waited to see you do that, Chance." I reckon that next to getting my revenge for Cora, seeing my oldest boy laugh like that was the best thing that had happened to me on this trip.

"Might surprise you, Pa, but I've been waiting on that my own self. All that shooting and killing and warring, it'll take it out of you. Strip your soul clean and make you wonder ary you'll ever be a whole man again."

Chance is a big man, so when he fell next to that cottonwood, well, hoss, I didn't bother moving him at all. No sir. I did my doctoring right there. He appeared in good spirits now, so I was gentle with him when I hoisted him up to a sitting position against the cottonwood as Wash brought over his food.

"Know what you mean, brother," Wash said, handing him a fork and holding his plate for him while Chance began to shovel food into his mouth. It crossed my mind that Wash was showing a genuine interest in taking care of his brother and that was good too. "You go off to fight a war that you sometimes ain't even sure of the meaning of it," he continued, shaking his head in despair. "Killing people you don't know just because they're wearing a uniform contrary to yours. It's a spooky feeling, I'll tell you.

"But you know something?" he said, a slow smile coming to his face. "What we done here was different. It had a genuine purpose to it and it didn't seem wrong or confusing or any of that. Strange, ain't it?"

"You don't suppose that would have anything to do

with being a part of a *family* again, do you?" I suggested, raising an eyebrow.

"I reckon it does," Chance said around a mouthful of food. "I always did know I could count on you two to watch my back when we went in guns drawn. Gives you a sense of security, even when you're going up against certain death."

"Couldn't have done what we did if it was anyone other than you two I had to rush this camp with. No sir," Wash said. "You and T. J. Faro."

After a moment of silence, Chance pushed his plate toward his brother. "Give me another helping of that stuff, along with the coffee, brother. I can feel my strength coming back."

What with Chance eating like he had a bottomless pit for a stomach again, I felt myself breathing easier, knowing the boy would soon be well.

We were lucky to have gotten away from this whole mess with just Chance being wounded. It could have been a whole different story, especially if I'd come alone.

"I'm glad you boys come along," I said after Chance had finished his second plate of beans in silence. Wash and I had poured some coffee and sipped at it while Chance ate. I reckon no man likes to eat alone in front of others, but coffee was the best we could do then. Besides, I don't think Chance would even have noticed who else was eating, he was that hungry.

"I'm glad you brought us along," Chance said and belched.

"He's getting better," Wash said with a smile. "When Chance makes sounds like that after he's through eating, why, you know there ain't nothing wrong with his insides. Just trying to get out of work now is what he's doing."

"Ain't that the truth," I said with a mock serious look that said I remembered days gone by when what Wash was saying wasn't far from the truth of it all. I reckon everyone has faults and my boys weren't any different from anyone else.

"If you boys hadn't come along, I'd have busted in here thinking I was another Jim Bowie and forgetting that I was at the Alamo," I said slowly. "I had no right to bring you along. I had no right to blame your mother's death on you two." It was as close as I'd ever come to apologizing to either of these boys of mine, and I'll admit it was a hard thing to do. Swallowing my pride never was one of my strong suits.

"Horse apples, Pa," Wash said, suddenly turning serious. "Believe me, I don't think Chance or me wanted to see any more dying than you did. But you know something, there was some good that come out of this trek we set out on. Hell, we're working like a family again, ain't we? Seems to me that if we didn't come along on this trip, why, we'd still be back there in Twin Rifles getting it all out of each other's systems and beating the bejesus out of one another. And I'll tell you, gents," Wash added, as though he had touched on a wisdom neither of us had thought of thus far. "Stubborn as this family is, why, we'd have gone at it tooth and nail until none of the three of us had any teeth left. And I'll guarantee you that Sarah Ann, Rachel, and Miss Margaret, why, none of the three of 'em would take us back!"

"The boy's right," Chance said with a smile. "Those women would give up cooking and baking for sure." Then his thoughts turned somber as he looked at me and said, "I think you're forgetting that one of the reasons we came along, Pa, was because she was our mother. We had a stake in avenging her too.

"You know, when I was out there, during the war, I used to remember that reading she had done for us as kids and how she read the Good Book to us. Every time I got through one of those battles alive, I'd look at all those dead men about me and remind myself that Ma had read a piece in the Good Book about the Lord giving and the Lord taking away. I reasoned that was his way of giving and taking, and my number just hadn't come around yet.

"But after seeing what I have out here, well, it changed my line of thought. Now, I ain't much of a churchgoer, Pa, but the way I figure it, why, if ma's death is how the Lord takes away, He'd be in disfavor with one helluva lot of people. No," he said, shaking his head in disbelief. "I figure that part about the Lord giving is likely right. But it's bastards like Terco and the rest of these bandidos that are the takers.

"Mind you, now, I won't forget what I done during that war, the killing and all. I reckon there's even some I'll regret. But you won't never see me spend a day of my life feeling sorry for what happened here. And if I remember it, and I'll remember it until the day I die, it'll only be because these sonsabitches were part and parcel to my mother's death.

"I wouldn't go apologizing for what you said or the way you feel, Pa," he said, a tone of sincerity now in his voice. I must confess that it was a tone I'd not heard before. "Looking back, I'd have said and done the same thing, were I in your place." He paused a moment, scratched his head in thought. But I knew he wasn't through speaking yet. "Strikes me that maybe T. J. Faro was right. Maybe we've been butting heads over who's right instead of what's right. Well, Pa, as far as I'm concerned, what we done here is what was right. And the rest of it don't matter. Not a-tall."

"Lordy, Chance," Wash said, "I ain't never heard you talk that long at a time."

"Me neither, Wash," I said, feeling a warmth spread through me that had been a long time in coming. "But he got the words right, and I reckon that's what counts."

He did and it was, and that was a moment amongst the three of us that I will never forget.

CHAPTER
★ 20 ★

I don't know whether it was all of that beans and Indian bread that did it or not, but Chance appeared to be considerably better the next morning, so it was on the fourth day that we set out back to Twin Rifles.

Even Chance admitted there wasn't much you could do with your arm in a sling, but he had that brand-new holster of his back at his side, so I reckon in part that made him feel like a man again. He wasn't peaked and he had his wits about him, so I figured I'd make use of him.

"You do much scouting in that war of yours?" I asked as we mounted up. Getting on a horse was still a bit of a chore for Chance, but he made it with only a short wince crossing his face.

"Some. What did you have in mind?"

"Well, boys," I said, addressing both of my sons now. "A man in this country has got to make do with what he can find, no matter what it was. Seems to me I taught you fellas something about that way back when." I scratched my head, as though thinking. "From what I've seen since you come back, why, I'd say you remembered that lesson right well."

"Then what are you repeating it for, Pa?" Wash asked.

"It also crossed my mind that you two might've forgotten it in all the excitement of late."

"Could be." Chance grinned. "What did you have in mind?"

"Well, it appears to me that this scum we just got through burying ain't got no use for all its earthly possessions."

Wash shrugged. "True."

"And you know good and damn well I ain't gonna scour the countryside looking for relatives 'cause in all likelihood these pilgrims ain't got any."

"Most of 'em looked like they got run into by the front end of one of them iron horses," Chance said, remembering the faces of some of the men, more than likely the ones he'd killed. A body never does seem to forget that. "Too ugly for a woman to take a liking to, at least when they're *that* ugly."

"Only woman ever loved 'em was likely their mama," Wash added, "and I'd have reservations about her."

"There's some good horseflesh here," I said. "The way I see it, Nathan Potts has got room in that livery of his to put these horses up. If I let him have a small commission for selling the horses for you, and throw in the saddles for free, why, I do believe he'd find you a buyer in no time.

174

"As for Kelly's Hardware," I added, turning my glance to Wash, "old Mike Kelly said he was thinking of expanding that gun rack behind his counter. You boys clean up these six-guns, rifles, and such, and you could sell 'em to Mike for five dollars each and both of you will wind up making a profit."

"Not to mention the fact," Chance said, "that ary we run into some trouble with the Comanches between here and Twin Rifles, we'll have enough guns and ammo to hold off half the nation."

"That too," I said, although I had to admit I hadn't been thinking about that aspect of having all this hardware with us. Maybe I am getting a mite old.

We followed the Pecos south, staying with the water as long as possible before we'd have to cross over and head back in the direction of Twin Rifles. It was the end of that first day that we came to the spot we'd first come upon the Pecos. We made camp, knowing that the following morning we'd be setting out across the Pecos and into a land that was nearly barren of water.

We found a couple of extra whiskey kegs that T. J. Faro had brought along with his pack mule. The whiskey was gone but the kegs were still good, so we rinsed them out with river water and filled them to the brim. We would need them for our trek across the back trail we were following. More specifically, the dozen horses we had were going to need the water. Maybe man doesn't live by bread alone, but neither do horses. It is water that a man will pay for or die for in a land like this. Fact of the matter is, he will not only pay or die for it for himself, but for his horse as well.

One thing I was sure of was the amount of supplies we had to get us across the land until we reached Twin Rifles. If we could keep ourselves in water for the next five to seven days and spread out the grain that remained for the horses, I was reasonably sure we'd have no trouble making it back home.

"Tell me something, Pa," Chance said that night as I panfried some thick slices of bacon.

"If I can." Like always I'd made the coffee first. A man's got to have coffee to survive in this land, I don't care what they tell you.

"This morning you said something about selling off all of these horses and guns for *us*. Just what did you have in mind?"

Whether they knew it or not, they were getting into a ticklish area when they took to talking finances. It's not that I was prying into their money matters, you understand, for no man likes that end of his affairs looked into by anyone. It's nobody else's business, as far as he is concerned. There was another matter that I hadn't spoken with my boys about yet, and it could be a downright personal matter too.

"Well, I just figured that you boys coming back from the war like you did, why, you didn't look like the richest men I'd ever seen."

"I see," Chance said. Wash was listening attentively.

I found myself pouring more hot coffee into my cup before I continued. I reckon T. J. Faro had an effect on me and the way I would do some things just as much as he had affected my boys.

I gulped down about half of that cup of coffee, burning my throat as I did, but somehow it didn't matter to me, not as much as what my boys would think of what I was about to say.

"The foundation on the old ranch house is still good," I started. "Don't know if you saw it that day I took you out there." I swallowed hard, but like I say, I wasn't even noticing the burn in my throat. "Clean it

176

up and all you'll need is some wood to take care of partitioning off the rooms on the inside. The adobe's still solid." If I sounded a mite humble, perhaps it was because I'd never be able to talk about that place without seeing Cora in my mind, and I don't mind telling you that it hurt something fierce. It was like my heart was breaking all over again, like I couldn't stop it and would never be able to.

"You thinking about rebuilding the old place?" Wash asked. "Is that what you're talking about?"

"Not for me, you understand," I said, feeling that hurt within me now. It was a hurt that saddened me. "I don't know that I could ever live there again. There're just too many memories there. But you boys—" I started to say, but words failed me. For the first time in I don't know how long, I was at a loss for words. Hell, that goes all the way back to the day I asked Cora to marry me. Took me all of one afternoon to work up the courage, and Cora to put the words in my mouth for me.

"Yeah." It looked like Chance was more fascinated with what was on my mind than he was angry, as I'd expected he would be. What the hell, might as well get it out in the open.

"You boys were off to a war," I said. "I don't know that I'll ever understand it, or that I'll ever want to understand it. But I've been to war my own self and I know there ain't nothing pretty about it, nothing at all. I've seen the way you boys handle yourselves since you've come back. Ary I ever had any doubts about you or how you fought in that war, well, I don't have 'em now. You two are as honorable a couple of gents as old T. J. Faro, no matter what uniform you wear. Maybe more so."

A look of pride came to Chance's face and I'd swear

I saw a good deal of me in the way he looked just then. It gave me a sense of pride too. He smiled and gave me a slap on the arm with his good hand. "Learned it from the best, Pa," he said.

"That's a fact, Pa," Wash said, looking mighty proud his own self. I had a notion those words were something they'd been waiting to hear ever since they'd returned. In a way, I felt kind of foolish for not seeing that need before now.

"It crossed my mind that you boys could put some work into that place and make a go of it ary you took a liking to it," I said. "Add on an extra room and you'd have living room for both your women when the proper time came.

"Hell, I reckon it's the best I can do to tell you boys I'm glad you made it back in one piece."

"I think I know what you mean," Chance said. Looking at him then it crossed my mind that my oldest son wasn't at all like the smart-alecky man who rode into Twin Rifles a week or two back. But then, I reckon we had all changed in that short amount of time.

"He's right, Pa," Wash said, taking the fry pan off the fire. "I think we both know what you mean."

"Hey!" Chance all but shouted upon seeing his brother dish out the now well-done bacon onto his plate. "What are you doing with my food!"

"Not this time, Chance," Wash said with a grin. To me he added, "Do you know this is the first time I've gotten to the food before him in I don't know how long? Fix your own, brother."

Things seemed to get back to normal after that. The night was quiet and each of the three of us spent most of it in silence before turning in, deep in our own thoughts. I know I slept well that night, and it wasn't because of exhaustion or the knowledge that I was in need of the rest. If anything, it was because I felt at peace with the world more than I had in a long time. I would never be able to forget the pain of Cora's death or the way it had happened, but I had avenged her and knowing that was as much as I could humanly do was enough to fill the void in me for a while. Added to that was the knowledge that I had two sons who I could be proud of, and being a father, well, I reckon there isn't much else you can ask of your boys as they grow older. No sir.

We got an early start the next morning and covered as much territory as we could until we found another water hole or the sunset. It was those days of moving across that barren land that I realized the importance of all of those landmarks that T. J. Faro had pointed out to us along the way. I had taught my boys to always watch your back trail, for things look different when you are going in the opposite direction. On the way back to Twin Rifles, one of the three of us was always able to spot one of the landmarks T. J. Faro had pointed out to us, and in so doing we were always near water when day's end came.

"Remind me to have a beer for T.J. when we get back to town," Chance said about the third day out. "He deserves it."

"Yeah," Wash agreed. Then, after a while he screwed up his face and said, "But ain't it spooky?"

"What's that?" I asked.

"The way he pointed all of this out to us. It was like he knew we were coming back but he wasn't. Otherwise he wouldn't have pointed it all out to us. Would he?"

"Could be," Chance said. "I got a notion Wash and me made T. J. Faro a tormented man."

"No," I said. "It wasn't you boys that tormented the man. It was a memory he couldn't get rid of in his mind. Don't go conjuring up guilt where there ain't none to be had, boys. It'll ruin your mind for a lifetime. Guaranteed."

It was noon of the seventh day that we rode into Twin Rifles, dusty, dirty, and thirsty enough to drink the well dry in one swallow. I reckon it was that preoccupation with getting a drink that kept us from noticing the obvious fact that something was wrong, something had changed. By the time I did notice, it was too late.

There were twenty, maybe twenty-five, blue-coated Yankee soldiers spread throughout town as we rode on through to Nathan Potts's livery stable. They looked awful satisfied, like some overstuffed pigs who'd been wallowing in mud. It was a look I didn't take to, and from the look of my boys, neither did they.

"Got some business for you, Nathan," I said as we dismounted. I took off my hat and wiped my brow, taking off a combination of sweat and dirt as I did. "Seems to be getting hotter every day, ary I'm any judge of the weather."

"Mister Will, that ain't half as hot as things been getting around *here,*" he said, his eyes nearly bulging out.

"He's right," a voice said from inside the barn. At first it was foreign, but by the time he stepped out in the open I recognized him. "Things have been sort of heated around here, although the weather had little to do with it."

It was Captain Alen and he was smiling as he spoke. But then, he was holding his Colt's Army Model .44 in his hand too. And he was pointing it right at us.

180

CHAPTER
★ 21 ★

"Don't give us any trouble, Marshal," Captain Alen said as a handful of his men appeared and stripped us of our handguns, knives, and rifles.

"You'll get no problem from me, Captain," Chance said. "All I want is for this wound to heal." What Chance said and the way he said it must have shocked Captain Alen, for Chance wouldn't have stood for it the last time he had seen the Yankee officer. No sir.

"Yes," the officer said, studying Chance. "It does look like you've been in a scrape, doesn't it?"

"What about the badges?" a man of fair proportions said. He was wearing sergeant stripes and looked tough enough and mean enough to hold the position. "Ain't no such thing as the Texas Rangers no more. And as for the marshal . . ." His voice trailed off and he wound up snorting in a derisive manner. I reckon it

181

was supposed to be a crude sort of laugh, but it didn't succeed. Sounded more like a wounded pig is what it sounded like.

"Very well, Sergeant Crawford, take them."

Sergeant Crawford decided then and there that I was going to be made some sort of example of for his commanding officer to see. Wanted to be some kind of hero, I reckon.

What he had in mind, I think, was to take hold of that marshal's badge of mine and tear it right off my shirt. He would have too, except for two things. First off, dirty as it was, the shirt I was wearing was one of my few good ones. Aside from that, well, I was wearing the shirt.

I grabbed hold of his wrist when he near had my badge in his grasp and pressed my thumb down over the vein as hard as I could. It took him by surprise, which is when I took *him* by surprise and laid a hard right alongside his jaw. The blow staggered him and he stumbled backward, but only so far as his arm would let him. I yanked the arm toward me and backhanded him so hard I do believe his family hurt. That blow staggered him too and this time I released the wrist and let him fall backward onto some horse apples.

No sooner had I taken a step toward him than two more Yankee uniforms appeared, one on each side of me, each pointing a six-gun at me. But I was consumed with hatred for the man I'd just knocked down and guns were the least of my worries. Tells you how much hatred can do to a body. Yes sir.

"Sonny," I growled mean as I looked, "I just got back from burying a dozen Daniel Boones who thought they were tough too."

"That's right," I heard Wash say in an offhand way.

"Drew five aces when they already had one showing. Bad practice, it is."

"Only person has anything to do with this badge is me. I take it off and I put it on." I stuck a stubby finger out at him as he got to his feet. "You try anything like that with me again and I'll kill you where you stand." Then I lowered my voice enough so only he and those near him would hear me when I said, "With my bare hands."

"Better put them things away, boys," Wash said to the two men with drawn guns. "He's been cantankerous all day, so I don't know ary he'd eat your guns by his own self or shove 'em down your throat. He's a hard man to gauge, Pa is."

The two gunmen gave each other odd looks then turned to the captain for direction. Wash had them a mite confused as to whether I was the reincarnation of Jim Bridger or just plain crazy, a little of both of which could be true.

"Nathan, I need to put these mounts up for a while," I said, all but ignoring the Yankee soldiers. "There's a good dozen of 'em here that'll bring a fair price if you can find a buyer for me. You get ten, twenty percent of the buy, whichever you think is fair. What do you say?"

"You got a deal," the big black man replied and heartily shook my hand.

"Good, I'll talk to you later. Right now I've got to get cleaned up. Come on, boys," I said and began to walk away, totally ignoring Captain Alen and his men.

I was either going to get shot in the back or yelled at, or I'd get away with it. I was so damned tired that I didn't think I'd feel it if they did shoot me. If they decided to yell at me, I'd likely go to war with the lot of them, just on principle.

It wasn't until we were a full block away that Chance all but busted out laughing at what we'd pulled off. Believe me, my boys know as well as I do that nobody likes to be ignored, especially when they're pointing something as dangerous as a six-gun at you and you act as though it isn't even there. I was hoping someone in town besides Nathan Potts had seen the confrontation me and my boys had with Captain Alen and his men, hoping maybe the word would get around that this Yankee could be bluffed.

Things weren't so good at my office, not if what Joshua started babbling about was even half-close to the truth.

"I tried, Will, I really did," he said in a voice that was more shame than humility. He was spitting out the words like we only had ten minutes before doomsday would be upon us.

"Whoa, now, Joshua," I said, taking in the darkened black of his left eye. Someone had landed a good one on Joshua's face and I was betting it wasn't from a fair fight of any sort. "It appears you walked into some sort of grizzly since I've been gone, but I reckon we'll get around to him. At least you're still walking and talking. Now settle down, son, settle down." I'd given thought about it one time and found myself running that same thought past me one more time now. Strange, isn't it, how we tend to treat some of the people we have a good respect for as though they were some sort of dog or horse of ours? Think about it the next time you're talking to an animal and then see if you don't talk near the same to a good friend. Maybe that's why a dog and a horse aren't all that far from being a man's best friend in this neck of the woods.

"Took the rifles and shotguns, they did," Chance

said, his sense of humor gone now as he surveyed the inside of my office.

"Damn sure did," Wash muttered. It was the first time I could remember hearing my youngest cuss in an offhand manner. But then, you take a man's guns out here and it's like stealing his horse from under him. A good horse, guns and ammo, and water were the essentials a man needed to survive in this land. Take one or all of them away and it was the same as raping him.

"They called me out onto the boardwalk a couple of days after you'd gone," Joshua said, still feeling ashamed of what had happened. "Like a fool, I took 'em up on it and stepped out of the office. That Captain Alen was out on the street, so I figured to keep an eye on him." His face flushed with red as he lowered his voice and said, "Damn, but I feel like a fool."

"Nonsense," I said to him. "You oughtta see what Chance walked into where we was at." It wasn't until he saw Chance flush his own self that Joshua began to believe me, I think.

"Pretty rough, was it?"

"And dry," I said, emphasizing the last word. "Why, Joshua, it was so dry out there, the fish in them streams was getting freckles." Whenever he'd felt bad like this before, I'd managed to lift Joshua's spirits by using his own sense of humor on him. My words brought a bit of a smile to his face now, and I found myself hoping it would settle him enough to bring out the rest of the story.

"Doesn't appear Alen was the one needed watching," Chance said.

"No, sir, Chance," Joshua confirmed. "That

185

Crawford fella, he'd got one helluva punch. Come at my flank from nowhere, he did." It was all falling into place now. They had bushwhacked my deputy, just as they had tried jumping me and my boys when we rode into town.

"Then it ain't your fault, Joshua," I said. "Man can only do so much."

"He's right," Wash said. "Why, you'd look plumb crazy with an eye stuck out each side of your head just so's you could watch both sides, Joshua. Plumb crazy!"

"I'll bet this Crawford decided it was time to collect your badge too, huh?" Chance said. He was picking up on things right quick now, Chance was.

"Yeah," my deputy said, sinking into his feeling of shame once again. "Sort of took over the town, it seems."

"Wait a minute, gents," Wash said, a bit of concern coming to him as he spoke. "What about the women?" His eyes drilled Joshua, as though holding him responsible for Sarah Ann's safety. "What about Sarah Ann?"

"And Rachel," Chance added with his own note of concern.

I felt like a fool for having gone this long and overlooking the safety of the women in town I was responsible for. "What about the women, Joshua? Are they all right?" I asked.

"Oh, they're fine," he replied. "I'd have told you boys right off ary something was wrong with 'em." I think all three of us Carstons breathed a sigh of relief about then.

"How come none of you have done anything about these yahoos yet?" I asked. This wasn't like the folks in Twin Rifles. They were all good honest people who wouldn't stand for riffraff of any sort in their town.

"Because of the women."

"I thought you said they were all right," Chance said in a frown.

"Oh, they are," Joshua said. "But this Captain Alen made it clear that ary anyone steps out of line, why, he'll turn loose his men on our women. It's bad enough they collected up all our guns. I don't think there's a man here who wants his woman taken by any of these heathens."

It was understandable. Under normal circumstances, I would likely have done the same thing. But I was the lawman in town and I was charged with taking care of the things that came up that were a mite out of the ordinary. And, hoss, this was a tad out of the ordinary. Yes sir. It was now up to me to come up with some solution to these soldiers who were occupying our town and acting like anything but soldiers.

"How many of them are there?" I asked Joshua.

"Two dozen near as I could count. Miss Margaret, why, she's madder than I'd ever thought I'd see a woman get! Taken over her whole boarding house, they have!"

"What!" Chance wasn't any too happy about what he'd just heard. I can't say that I was either.

"The *whole* boarding house?" Wash said in amazement.

"That's what I said." Joshua nodded in the affirmative.

"Seems to me we had rooms at that place, Pa," Chance said.

"That's a fact, son," I said and sloshed on my hat.

"Where you going?" Joshua asked as I headed for the door.

"You stay here, Joshua," Chance said, putting his dusty hat on and following Wash out the door behind me. "I got a notion that if you hear glass busting, it's gonna be Pa's St. Louis glass, and some sorry ass soldier is gonna be going through it."

CHAPTER
★ 22 ★

I may have had a hitch in my git along, hoss, but I had a fire that was building in my mind that was making up for any shortcomings I might otherwise have. Putting any of the ladies of Twin Rifles in danger was enough to give me the feeling of a man with a mission, just like I'd felt tracking down Terco and his crowd.

Lest you think I was walking into a confrontation with a goodly number of these Yankee soldiers without a weapon, I made certain to grab hold of that gnarled old walking stick of mine when I left my office. I only looked over my shoulder once to see whether either of my boys was following me, and felt a might foolish about doing that, for although they were grown men they were still following me around like so many pups, just like they had in their youth. And, just like they had in their youth, they both had that look about them that said they were curious as could be to see what their daddy was going to do now.

I all but tore off the door to Margaret Ferris's boarding house as I made my way through the entrance. Motivated? Shoot, son, I don't think they'd let you use words like I was thinking in the same room with a woman! But for a moment the thought was out of my mind, for Margaret, rushing to the front to see what the noise was, no sooner saw me than she was in my arms. Rachel was right behind her, rushing to meet Chance as he followed me through the doorway.

"Well, now, would you look at this," Wash said, standing there alone. "I wonder if Sarah Ann's got the same kind of welcoming committee ready for me?"

"Believe me, Wash, she does," Rachel said when she turned Chance loose.

"Rachel's right, G.W.," Margaret said with a smile. "Sarah Ann's been over here just about every day you've been gone."

Over my shoulder I saw my youngest pushing his hat back on his head and laying a finger to the back part of his thick yellow-brown hair, as though that one spot was where his brain was and he needed to do some digging to get it operating like some panhandle miner.

"That don't make an awful lot of sense," he said after a moment. "Why would she come over here if she knew I wasn't here to begin with?"

"Boy," I said in disbelief, "sometimes you purely mystify me."

"It's a woman's way, Wash," Chance said, glancing at his brother, then Margaret and Rachel, and then back to Wash again. "When the men are away, they get together and plot on how to take over the world."

"I'm going to remember you said that, Chance Carston," Rachel said in mock fury.

"I'm glad to see you back in one piece, Will," Margaret said with a longing look in her eyes. It was that same longing look I'd seen in her eyes when I'd left, and somehow it felt good to know that it hadn't changed all the time I'd been gone.

"Never had any doubts about coming back," I smiled. "However, I did manage to attract about half the dust in west Texas in the process."

"What we're needing, ladies," Chance said, "is a good home cooked meal along with a change of clothes and a hot bath."

"Oh, my," Margaret said, as though suddenly remembering a difficulty that would stand in her way.

"Joshua told us about Alen and his men taking over your place," I said with a frown. I headed for the stairs, stopped at the first step and looked back at Margaret. "You might say we come to undo a part of it, at least for the rooms us Carstons have got." I gave her a wink and a nod before climbing the stairs.

"Be careful, Will," I heard her say in a pleading voice. "They're—"

"I *know* what they are, Margaret," I said without looking back.

I didn't bother to knock. Hell, it was my room! But the door wasn't locked, so I had no trouble gaining entry.

"Hey! What the hell do you think you're doing!" a pint-size man said, chomping on an unlit cigar. You'd think he fancied himself another U. S. Grant so disheveled was his uniform. His partner, with whom he was playing cards, looked much the same, more from a way of life than on purpose. A smell of sweat that could only have been equaled by my own permeated the room.

"Game's over, boys," I said, pulling back the left vest of my coat to reveal my marshal's badge.

"The hell you say!" Shorty said, getting fired up real fast. "Captain Alen's the law here now!"

"Not hardly, sonny." I won't tell you that I was taking pleasure in being a lawman again. Maybe it was just that, after having tangled with those Comancheros, being scared of a bunch of filthy pilgrims like this didn't even cut the mark anymore.

Shorty decided it was time to start acting like U. S. Grant too, but he never got the chance. I brought my cane sideways across his chest and all but knocked him back onto the floor in the process.

"You get up lessen I tell you to, sonny, and I'll take out your teeth like no dentist you ever imagined could next time." To Filthy, I said, "You even think about moving and I'll tar and feather you just to get rid of the stink.

"Now, gents, this is my room and I come to collect the rent, not to mention evict you. Dig deep and lay out the color of your money. I'll tell you when to stop."

Between the two of them, they came up with all of twenty dollars and change before breaking the bank. I took all but the change gladly and told them to light a shuck and be quick about it.

"Mister, that's a good month's rent you've got there," Shorty said, although he had given up his U. S. Grant impersonation. "We only been here two weeks."

"True, but I'm gonna have to wait for a good Texas norther to blow enough air through this window to fumigate this room before I can live in it again. Now git before I make good on my promise."

With that they left. I was sure that they would be heading straight to Captain Alen with their complaint, which was fine with me, for I had a few thoughts jostling around inside my head now too.

In the hallway, I heard a thud. Stepping out from my doorway, I saw another bluecoat lying on the floor, half-in and half-out of Chance's room. He got up and began to walk back into the room. But his frame didn't get past the door before he came flying back out again, nearly falling over the rail that separated him from a long fall into the library room Margaret had opened for her guests. The man felt his jawline, then looked up in terror as Chance came charging out of the room, quickly backhanding the man. I'd nearly forgotten that his left arm was in a sling and that he only had one useful arm now. But he was making good use of it, I'll give him that.

"I'd leave while I can, son," I said, adopting Wash's tactic of butting into a good fight. "Mean as old Chance is, why, I figure his next move is to take that sling off, and then you'll really be in trouble."

I reckon the man believed me, for he took off running like a bat out of hell down the hallway, down the stairs, and out the door.

"Ouch! That hurts!" came the cry from the next room. Out came another reluctant boarder, wincing as though he had just broken his arm, and maybe he had. Wash had a firm grip on the man's arm, holding it tightly and to the center in back of him, pulling higher with each step the man took. "You're breaking my arm!"

"Now you've got the idea," Wash said, although I

wouldn't say he looked all that complimentary. Piss ugly mean was more like it, if you ask me.

"Ain't you being a mite harsh on him?" Chance said, seeing the same look I did on his younger brother.

"Sonofabitch is lucky I don't kill him here and now," Wash hissed, yanking the man's hand higher behind him as he pushed him down the hallway. At the top of the stairway, he yelled, "Coming through!" and gave the man a shove, sending him tumbling down the stairs like a tumbleweed, rolling over and over until he reached the bottom.

"You may have killed him, son," I said when the body stopped at the bottom of the stairs but didn't move.

"If not, I'll finish the job," he said, seething. He was dead set on doing just that, but Chance grabbed him with his one good hand and pushed him against the wall.

"What in hell's got you so fired up?" Chance said, asking what I was wondering my own self.

"Bastard said he was gonna take up with that whore worked over in the café!" Wash spit out the words like so much venom, but they were far more poisonous than any rattler I'd seen of late. "He called Sarah Ann a whore!"

"Don't blame you one bit," Chance said, letting go of his brother's arm.

The body at the bottom of the stairs was slowly moving now as one of the soldier's compatriots helped him up. With the massive amount of pain showing on his face, I'd no doubt the man had at least a broken arm, if not more. Still, he managed to throw a hateful look Wash's way, as though to say in all that silence that he would be waiting for Wash some day;

somehow he would get him for this. Of all the men we'd run out of our rooms that afternoon, I had a strong notion the one Wash had encountered was the one with a strong sense of pride.

Fifteen minutes later we had shucked our clothes and had each climbed into a tub of hot water downstairs in the room Margaret kept available for such things. What made it all the better was that we could smell the odor of food being prepared and knew that Rachel and Margaret were doing it just for the three of us. I tried out a few of the ideas I had rattling around in my brain, thinking some more on how I was going to take care of Captain Alen and his Yankee troops. I would have thought more, but I got interrupted by Captain Alen himself.

"I understand you've been making trouble for some of my men," he said, when he threw back the curtain to our room and stood before us. I had the distinct impression that he liked looking down on people, for he stood before us now with his hands on his hips, like some overbearing father about to thrash his disobedient sons.

"You know, Captain," I said, getting a wee bit mad at the interruption, "you've got this strange idea that you're running this town, and that just ain't so."

"No, Carston," he said defiantly, *"you're* the one who thinks he's running this town." He would have said more, but all of a sudden he flinched and I thought I saw the glint of a knife poke him from the side next to the entrance way.

"Captain Alen," I heard Margaret's firm voice say, "I couldn't care less about who runs this town." She must have pushed her butcher knife a mite harder into the man's side, for he flinched some more as a worried look came to his face. "But I think you should know that *I* run this boarding house, and I don't allow anyone in back of the dining area." Her voice was getting stronger and harder as she spoke, helped along a little I reckon by the fact that she had a razor sharp knife in her hands. "Now, unless you want to find out how good I am with this butcher knife, I suggest that you very quietly and very quickly remove yourself from this area."

Captain Alen's flinch turned into a surprised look of pain as he moved a step to the right, then quickly did as he was told. I wouldn't be surprised at all if he was feeling a tad bit of warm liquid in his side that last time. But then, knowing you've been cut does things to your bravado, not to mention your energy.

The curtain fell back in its place and I heard the scurry of Margaret's little feet back to her kitchen area.

"Well, now, Pa," Chance said with a smile, "you think Miss Margaret's taking a liking to you? Seems like she saved our bacon."

Before I could answer, Wash put his two cents worth in. "Of course not, Chance. Miss Margaret got that captain out of here because she didn't want to let all that good food her and Miss Rachel are making go to waste. It's pure and simple reasoning, it is."

Chance shook his head in disbelief. "Pa, you've got to talk to this boy."

"I know, Chance. I know."

It must have been around three or four o'clock by the time we got dressed and sat down to eat. By the way our stomachs were growling, why, you'd have thought we hadn't eaten in a week. Of course, the truth of the matter was that it had been upward of two weeks or more since we'd had cooking like that of Margaret and Rachel. The roast they had prepared was sliced good and thick. The coffee was hot, as were the biscuits, piled high on a large plate. The potatoes were fried to a golden brown. In between the two plates was a bowl of butter, which I expected would surely melt from the heat surrounding it.

The only thing that made it all that much better was glancing up occasionally to see the proud smiling faces of Margaret and Rachel Ferris, taking us in while we devoured their food. I could remember my mother taking such pride in fixing a setting for my daddy and the rest of the family. I reckon it is some sort of built-in motherly instinct that women develop for the men in their lives. A man goes to building a shelter for his woman and she takes care of him as best she can, for she knows he's breaking his back for her and her alone. Feeding him good and proper is about the best way she can keep him going. Oh, there are other ways, but those are a whole lot different and a whole lot more private. If you know what I mean.

"Ladies, you set a fine table," I said with a satisfied belch when I pushed away my plate and accepted more coffee.

"Man's right," Chance said. "My stomach's been yearning for this kind of meal ever since we left town."

"How about some apple pie?" Margaret suggested.

"I'll bite," Chance said. I noticed that he tended to get real feisty around Rachel since he'd returned from the war.

"Somehow, I thought you'd say that." I think she was noticing too.

When the women left the room, I glanced at my boys.

"Somehow or other we're gonna have to fashion a way to get these Yankees out of Twin Rifles."

197

"Ain't that the truth."

"It's gonna be hard to catch 'em off guard, Pa," Chance said. "There's twice as many of them as those Comancheros we dealt with, so surrounding them is gonna be tough."

Margaret and Rachel returned, carrying a steaming apple pie and three plates. Setting it before us, they went to work dividing up the pie.

"By the way, Will," Margaret said, "are you ready to give your usual speech tomorrow?"

"Ma'am?" She'd caught me off guard, but then, that is like most women.

"Don't be silly, Will," she said in that way women have of making you look like a fool, whether they're trying to or not. "Tomorrow's the Fourth of July, remember?"

"Well, I'll be," I said to myself. She could have hit me over the head with a good two-by-four and not gotten my attention in any better manner. Suddenly, all of those ideas I had been toying with all afternoon were coming together into one big plan.

"What're you thinking, Pa?" Chance must have seen the look in my eye.

"I'm thinking we're gonna get rid of these damn Yankees after all." Things were racing through my mind, and they required a lot of preparation. "Rachel, I want you to go to the front door and grab the first boy you see and tell him I want to see him and all his friends as soon as possible."

"What'll I tell them?"

"You tell 'em this meeting's gotta be secret. Tell 'em ary they can pull off what I've got in mind, I'll supply each one of 'em with enough penny candy to keep 'em sick for a good week!"

Margaret's daughter shrugged and set off to follow

my directions. Margaret set out three plates of pie, but Wash pushed his away.

"No offense, Miss Margaret, but it's time I visited Sarah Ann," he said, his face beaming as he slapped on his hat.

"But don't you want any dessert?"

"That's what I'm going for, ma'am. Dessert."

"Pa, you're gonna have to talk to that boy," Chance said.

"I know, Chance. I know."

CHAPTER
★ 23 ★

It was all set.

By sunset that night I had those youngsters running their tails off this, that, and the other way, setting my little game in motion. They slept well that night, those boys, but they were up by sunrise the next morning.

"They'll be coming in later this morning, Mister Will," young Johnny said, out of breath that Fourth of July morning as I ate my breakfast.

"Good," I said, feeling a sense of civic pride. "I'm glad you told me those Tyler boys were back from the war, Johnny. They always were reliable folks."

"Do you really think they'll fall for it, Pa?" Wash asked, working on his second cup of coffee.

"Never you mind, G.W.," Margaret said with confidence. "If Will says it'll work, why, it'll work, you can bet on it." Her words brought a smile to my face and a calm sort of reassurance to my heart. Somehow, it was good having someone of the opposite persuasion believing in you; it made a difference sometimes. Yes sir.

I'd thought it all out the day before, after Wash had gone to see Sarah Ann. Sometimes things just fall into place, and that afternoon had been one of those times.

Like Chance had said, we would need to circle this crowd just like we did those Comancheros, but that was going to be mighty tough considering we didn't have any guns and there were twice as many of these Yankees as there had been Comancheros. That left us our wits to work with to overcome these fellows. And using my head for more than a place to set my brand-new John B. Stetson was exactly what I did that afternoon.

What we were needing was something to cut the odds, and that was when T. J. Faro's comments about whiskey being poison came to mind. I sent young Billy to the saloon with word that tomorrow the saloon should open promptly at ten o'clock, an hour earlier than usual. Every Yankee was to be given whiskey at half price. And if they asked, well, what the hell, son, it was the Fourth of July . . . drink on up!

I figured that two hours of steady drinking would be enough to give these yahoos a fuzzy-eyed look at the world. It was the poison that would cut the odds more to our liking. By noon I was going to be making my annual Fourth of July speech and would invite these Yankees to listen in on it.

If my boys had done their jobs proper, nearly all of the town proprietors would be making their way to my speech, circling these Yankees if they did it right.

That's where I hit a dead damn halt.

"How in the hell are we gonna take 'em?" Chance said, running the question past me that I'd asked my own self at least a hundred times by now. "They've got the guns! What in blazes are we gonna do, Pa?"

"I don't know, Chance, but one way or another we've got to try to get Captain Alen and his pilgrims out of our town."

"Why don't you fight 'em?" Johnny said, raising a fist. "Bam!" he said, slamming it down into the opposite hand. "That's what you always tell me you did when you're story telling, Mister Will. Go right up to 'em and beat the living daylights outta 'em! Yes, sir," he said with a wink and a nod. By God, the boy reminded me of me.

"I know, Johnny," I said, trying to explain myself without sounding too much the fool. "But you see, son, well that's just story—"

"Telling, based on fact," Chance interrupted. "That's right, Johnny, Pa wouldn't lead you astray. No sir, son, when he tells you that's how it's done, why, you can bet that's how it's done." Chance had stunned all of us with his words. Pushing himself from the table, he put on his hat and gave Johnny's tousled hair a brush as he headed for the door. "You just watch what happens today, Johnny, and you'll get a first-rate example of how accurate Pa's story telling is."

"Now, what was that all about?" Wash said in bewilderment, scratching the part of his brain that got his curiosity going.

"I don't know," I said, just as confused, "but it sure made me feel awful good, whatever it was."

Chance never did come back that morning to

explain his words. Or maybe he did and I didn't notice him. All I remember was drinking close to another pot of coffee trying to figure out how to resolve the dilemma I was in. Hell, the dilemma the town was in.

How do you get a bunch of unarmed middle-age men to go up against a crowd of Yankees who looked all too anxious to use their guns? It was pushing noon when it came to me. Of course, when it did, I felt like the damnedest fool who ever walked the earth, for it had been there right before me all the time.

I made my way to my office, in search of the book I pulled out once a year, every Fourth of July, and put away until the following year. Glancing through it, I wondered if a body shouldn't take it out more often to read, perhaps more often to ponder the meaning of its words. I knew I had precious little time to do that now, but I made quick business of it, fearful that I would miss giving my speech.

Leaving the marshal's office, I spotted the five Hadley brothers riding into town. They all had six-guns but they all turned them over to the Yankee guards at Kelly's Hardware Store they pulled up in front of. Handed those guns over without so much as a fight too. Now, hoss, that was strange.

What was stranger was how they entered the hardware store and did so quietly. I say that because the Tyler boys had their horses tied to the hitch rack outside the hardware store, and these two clans had been fighting one another worse than my boys had in their youth. Something was going on and it struck more than my curiosity that it was something I didn't know a damn thing about either.

Johnny had hauled a dusty old podium in front of the Ferris House and was ringing a bell for all to gather as I crossed the street. Like I figured, about three quarters of those Yankee bluecoats were the better part of drunk as they approached the podium. The trouble was not *all* of them were there, and that could put a hitch in my plans, if they materialized.

Most of the townsfolk must have gotten the word my boys had sent out, for I thought I saw damn near all of them coming out of their stores just like I'd planned. Mind you, now, if any of those soldiers had a brain, why, they would have figured out that if this was a holiday the stores would be closed, right? But not these pilgrims. Their minds were in such a stupor that they didn't know or care. This was just another formation they were being called to attend.

"As most of you know, this is the Fourth of Ju y," I started, only to hear a couple of grumbles in the audience. "I'll grant you, now, this ain't like holidays of the past. But I want you folks to think on something, for this ain't gonna be one of those Fourth of Julys you're likely to ever forget."

"How we gonna do that?" one resident said. "Can't have a Fourth of July without no fireworks, and I don't see any promise of none to come."

"We'll see about that, my friend," I said. "But first I want you to know something." I paused a moment before lifting one of my prized possessions, a leather bound copy of the Constitution of the United States of America. "The contents of this book is what we celebrate this day of the year, each and every year. Pull it out, dust it off, and take a gander at a title that assures us that we are still the freest nation in the world.

"But it strikes me that we ought to take note of just what the contents of this Constitution are. For instance . . ." I thumbed through my book until I'd found the page I'd marked and began to read:

Amendment I
Congress shall make no law respecting an establishment of religion, or prohibiting the free exercise thereof; or *abridging the freedom of speech,* or of the press; or the right of the people peaceably to assemble, and to petition the Government for a redress of grievances.

Amendment II
A well-regulated militia, being necessary to the security of a free State, *the right of the people to keep and bear arms, shall not be infringed.*

Amendment III
No soldier shall, in time of peace be quartered in any house, without the consent of the owner, nor in time of war, but in a manner to be prescribed by law.

Those of the soldiers who could make out what I was saying nodded and agreed with one another about these words of wisdom. The people I shared the town of Twin Rifles with were making the same noises, but with a more intense attitude. I thought I knew why.

"I won't bother you with reading all the rest of them," I continued. "You can do that any time you'd like to borrow my book here. Ary you've got your own copy, so much the better.

"I did read those first three amendments because I believe they have a definite meaning to the people of Twin Rifles. Freedom of speech, the right to bear arms, and a couple of notes on soldiers and what they're allowed and not allowed to do, be it peace or war."

I knew then how I was going to do it, knew how I would get these folks to take back their town. Chance must have seen it back when I was talking to Johnny. Hell, maybe I'm getting old. I don't know. I did know I was feeling mighty proud about being an American right then. Yes sir, mighty proud.

"Folks, I'm here to tell you that I don't think we oughtta put up with the likes of these Yankees, not one damn day more! And, by God, there's only one way we're gonna rid Twin Rifles of 'em!"

A door bursting open interrupted my speech as Carny Hadley came tumbling out of Kelly's Hardware Store. Chance wasn't far behind him, cussing up a storm something fierce. For that matter, Wash, the rest of the Hadley boys, and the Tyler boys as well, all followed the two out into the street. What with Kelly's Hardware being directly across the street from the Ferris House, why, the lot of them managed to open up the center of my audience so they had some room.

"You can't talk about my Rachel like that, Carny," Chance said loud enough for the whole town to hear before hitting the older Hadley ass over teakettle again.

All attention turned to Chance and Carny now. As soon as it did, I saw the whole thing. I saw all that Chance had in mind. By God, maybe there was some hope for me and my feeble brain yet!

"Boys! Boys! Boys!" I yelled out at the top of my lungs until I had their attention once more. Even Chance and Carny had stopped to listen.

"Yes, yes, Carston," one man said impatiently. "Speak your piece and be done with it."

"There's only one way we're gonna get rid of these damn Yankees, and that's the same way the boys at Bunker Hill did with those redcoats, even with the odds against 'em."

I could have been talking to school children who had never had a lesson in history before, the lot of them looked that dumbfounded. It was almost as if seeing Chance and Carny Hadley going at it heel-and-toe had grabbed their complete attention and they had completely forgotten what I'd been speaking about. When they all shared a few heavy seconds of silence, well, hoss, that tore it!

"Damn it!" I yelled impatiently. I must have looked like a madman waving my fist behind that podium. "You wanted fireworks. Fight 'em!" I yelled again, this time sweeping my arm before me so it would take in all of the bluecoats in the streets.

Joshua was the first one to see what I meant and jumped the big sergeant, Crawford, bowling him over in the dust. Attention turned from Chance to Joshua as my deputy began to beat the tar out of the sergeant he had caught off guard. Oh, the man was bigger all right, but righting a wrong always does add a touch of fury to a man's being, and Joshua proved he had that. He kept swinging at Crawford until the man's face was nothing more than blood and bruises and he fell to the ground unconscious.

"There's a lot more of 'em over here, folks," I heard Chance yell from his spot in the middle of the crowd.

"That's right, folks," Carny Hadley said, now standing by Chance's side as though he were his best friend, "today you get to make your own fireworks."

I don't think they saw it right away, the ruse that Chance and Carny had put on to grab everyone's attention, but when they did there was no stopping them. What made them see the truth of the matter was, well, the truth of the matter.

The whole fight started with Chance and Wash fighting back-to-back alongside the five Hadley boys and the three Tyler brothers. Mind you now, this was a sight to behold, for the boys in these three families had grown up fighting one another in their youth. And here they were now fighting off a bunch of intruders and doing it back-to-back like they all belonged, which they did.

I reckon I'd made the same mistake a lot of folks did who had boys coming home from the war. I figured that since they lost, why, they were cowards, and that turned out to be far from the truth. The fact of the matter was, these boys had all come home from being at war for two, three, or four years, and had survived. You can't call any man who has the guts to fight for what he believes in a coward. That was just what those boys turned men were doing now in the streets of Twin Rifles. Oh, they may have lost a war, but they hadn't lost pride in being who they were, and being willing to take on a bunch of roughshod Yankees who were in the wrong no matter how you sliced it, why, that was no act of cowardice. No sir. Truth is, I was feeling my chest swell up a mite as they lit into those damn Yankees. I'm proud to say the rest of my town, the rest of Twin Rifles, started feeling the same way.

Chance only had one good arm, but he made damn good use of it, with Wash giving him a hand when he needed it. Seeing that, well, it gave me pause to know that I'd done something right in bringing up those boys. Yes sir.

One Yankee decided it was time to put Chance out of commission and hit him hard as he could on his left shoulder, which was still in a sling. He made one hell of a mistake.

"Damn it, that hurt!" Chance yelled, a look of pain crossing his face. But it wasn't the pain so much as the mad that was building in my son now as he turned to the smart ass who had hit him. Everyone who saw it knew what was going to take place, except for the fellow it was going to happen to, I reckon. Wash had moved around to the man's side and stuck a foot out behind him. At the same time, Chance hauled off and hit the man, likely twice as hard as he had hit Chance. What with Wash's foot behind him, why, that fellow went down faster than a tin can at a shooting match.

Big John Porter, Sarah Ann's father, didn't need a butcher knife or that Colt's Dragoon of his. He simply waded into the mass of swinging arms and grabbed a couple of bluecoats by the neck and knocked their heads together. After that he simply looked about for anyone from Twin Rifles who looked like he'd taken on more than he should and lent a hand, mostly cracking heads.

Some of the women even got mixed up in this foray, hitting bluecoats with everything from broom handles to the heavy iron skillet I saw Rachel lay up alongside one fellow's head. He took to napping right early that day. But the woman who surprised me most that day was Margaret.

Captain Alen didn't take kindly to Joshua beating the living tar out of what he likely considered his best sergeant. I reckon the man was too much of a coward to fight him heel-and-toe, so he pulled out his pistol and was about to shoot my deputy when I heard a shot go off to my rear. It made me jump, for I wasn't expecting it.

Captain Alen fell to the ground, wounded. Margaret stepped to my side, an old Navy Colt's in her hand, near ready to cry. I doubt that she'd ever done such a thing before.

"It's the old pistol you said you left for Cora," she explained. "I took it from your trunk when they said they were going to confiscate all the firearms in town. I hid it."

"I'm glad you did, darlin'," I said. "You just saved Joshua's life."

"Will!" she yelled. I'd faced her briefly after she fired the shot, but she was still looking out over the fight scene. All I needed to see was the terror in her eyes to know that something wasn't right.

"Joshua!" I yelled not a second after I turned to see Captain Alen cocking and readying his pistol for the one shot he would need to kill my deputy. Margaret had knocked him down but he wasn't out of the fight yet. She had hit him in the side and he was bleeding something fierce, most likely dying.

"Captain!" I yelled, this time hoping to divert him. It worked and I had his attention as he swung his gun around to try to kill me instead.

Just like T. J. Faro, I'd learned a few things in my day. One of them was to keep an ace in the hole, and I used mine now. When I'd made my gnarled old piece of wood for a walking stick, I'd also seen a prime knife maker and had him fit the handle with a good throwing blade. One good yank on the top of the handle and out came that knife, all six inches of the blade shining in the noon light. I turned sideways as the captain shot, hitting me in the arm and knocking me back, but I was able to regain some sort of balance before he could fire again. I threw that knife as hard as I could and hit my target, driving the knife blade to the hilt into the Yankee captain's heart. If he wasn't dead before he fell to the ground, he damn sure ought to have been.

My arm hurt like hell, but I managed to stay on my feet.

The fight was getting to be more than some of those troops could take and they started looking for ways to get the hell out of there. Two of the bluecoats who hadn't made it to the meeting now mounted their horses and made a run for it. The whole thing was turning into a losing proposition and they made a quick decision to call it quits.

"Wash! Quick! Get a rifle and stop those two!" I yelled above the noise of the fight.

I needn't have done that, for as the two riders began to race out of town, they met up with Nathan Potts, who stepped out from his livery stable, shotgun in hand. The rider on his near side was blown from his saddle by one blast, but I saw Nathan take a shot from the second rider as the man continued his ride out of town.

Wash pulled a Spencer rifle from the scabbard of one riderless horse as he ran as fast as he could toward Nathan's livery. I did the best I could to make my way to Nathan as well.

At the edge of town, Wash stopped, took a deep breath, aimed his rifle and fired a shot that seemed to hang in the air for some time. Finally, the rider jerked forward and fell from his saddle.

"He's dead," Wash said with certainty.

"How do you know?" one onlooker asked.

Wash looked at me and smiled. "Practice," he said, knowing that I'd remember his shooting of the one Comanchero who tried to escape not a week earlier.

"Take his word for it, Charlie," I said.

211

Then I saw Nathan lying there, still gripping his shotgun in one hand, holding the other over a bullet hole in his chest that couldn't be dammed up. I realized then that he was one of my best friends and he was dying and I couldn't do a damn thing about it. I found myself cussing out loud and not caring who heard me as I knelt down on one knee and took the scattergun from the black man's hand.

"I sure didn't figure this for a good day for dying," he said, trying to smile as he spoke.

"There ain't no good days for dying, Nathan," I said, feeling anger and remorse at the same time and wondering if that was humanly possible. "Now shut up and rest."

He was silent for a moment, then coughed and spit blood from his mouth. When he looked past me, I glanced over my shoulder and saw Chance lumber on over toward us.

"You sell them hosses to the army, Chance," he said, speaking for a bit as though nothing had happened. It sent an eerie feeling shivering through me, for I knew he was a dying man and so did he. "They give you a good price.

"What's the matter, Wash?" he asked, smiling at my youngest son, who was running his arm across his upper lip.

"Tain't fair, Nathan." I do believe the boy was about ready to cry. "Every time I've met up with a hero, he always winds up dead. Tain't fair."

"Shoot, boy. Why, you the hero. You betcha, boy."

The words took a lot out of him and I think he knew that the end wasn't far off. Hell, I'd seen men like Nathan Potts die before. Somehow, you always knew when it was near.

He was silent for a moment before grabbing hold of

my hand. I could tell by the way he held on that it wouldn't be long now.

"Not many of my kind *live,* Will, but I did. For thirty years I *lived* and that's something. You'll put the letters on my marker, won't you, Will?"

"Wouldn't have it any other way, Nathan," I said and then he died.

"Letters?" one onlooker asked in bewilderment. "What letters?"

"F.M.C.," Chance said in a hard voice, as though he couldn't stand the ignorance of the man. "Free Man of Color."

Now there were bluecoats lying all over the place, the bodies in them stretched out on the main street of Twin Rifles. Standing over them were middle-age men who had gained a new sense of pride because today, the Fourth of July, they had fought for their freedom and won. Along with them stood our children who were no longer our children, for they had gone off to war and had grown up hard and fast and, in more than one case, mean when the occasion called for it. They may not have won the war they had gone off to, for there are no real winners in war, only survivors, but they had just proved to themselves and their fellow townsmen that they could both take it and dish it out.

I think we all knew that this wasn't just the Fourth of July in the year of our Lord 1865. For many of us it was a homecoming and a day we'd not soon forget.

CHAPTER

★ 24 ★

The rest of that Fourth of July turned out to be relatively quiet compared to what went on in the way of fireworks. Chance and I got our wounds looked at and patched up. According to the doctor, we'd be mighty sore and a tad weak for a few days. Losing blood will do that to you, I reckon. But it was the day after the Fourth that things got back to normal, or at least the way they should be.

I sent Joshua to the nearest military installation as an escort for the dead Yankee captain and the scoundrels he called his men. Since there were two dozen of them, I swore in the Hadleys and Tylers to go along and keep an eye on these yahoos.

"Now, remember, boys," Joshua said, talking the part of a man of importance now that he was chief honcho of the outfit. "These are the fellers we're fighting, understand?" he said, tossing a thumb over his shoulder at the bluecoats behind him.

"Don't worry, Joshua," Carny Hadley said. "Hell, the war's over."

"I know," my deputy said suspiciously, "but you fellers are still brothers, and that makes me awful curious about any of you burying the hatchet except in one another's back."

"You boys behave," I said, as though being a father to the whole lot rather than a lawman. Sometimes I wonder what the difference is, if any. "By the by," I added, "I'd appreciate it if a couple of you boys would stop by Nathan Potts's livery and take those dozen mounts we brought back with us. If Nathan said the army was needing 'em and giving a good price for 'em, then that's the way it is. Carny, you're a pretty good haggler. Why don't you see can't you get a better than fair price for 'em and I'll pay you better than average for 'em?"

"You've got a deal, Mister Carston."

"Johnny," I said to the youngster who'd largely been responsible for helping get the town back, even if in an indirect manner, "why don't you show Carny which ones I'm talking about?"

"You bet, Mister Will."

"There's one other thing I want you to take care of, Joshua," I said before he left with his prisoners.

"Name it."

I handed him a letter. "You give this to the commander in charge of that fort. It's a list of my St. Louis glass that these yahoos busted up. You tell that fella I've already put replacement glass on order and I by God expect the United States goddamn Army to pay for it! You tell him ary he don't agree to that, why, he'll likely have to deal with the better share of the residents of Twin Rifles when they come to take over his fort."

Joshua smiled. "I'll tell him *just* that, Will."

Later that morning, we all attended funeral services for Nathan Potts. It's never easy burying a friend. It was that day that I realized that I'd never really thought of Nathan as a colored man. He had always been a man and that was that.

On the way back from the cemetery, the memory of T. J. Faro came to mind and for the life of me I couldn't understand why. All the way back to the boarding house I thought of T.J. and those days we'd spent together before we'd come upon the Comancheros. By the time we reached the boarding house, I thought I knew why he had come to mind.

Margaret and Rachel and Sarah Ann had been all gussied up, if that's what you call dressing for a funeral. And just between you and me, hoss, I've got to tell you that there is a strange correlation between life and death. I say that because Margaret sure did look inviting. I don't know if realizing how frail and short life really is what made me want her, or the fact that some of those skimpy girls from the red-light districts of the larger towns dressed with a shade of black as well. Still, it was the memory of T. J. Faro that lingered with me the strongest that day.

"If you boys can wait about half an hour, why, we'll have a nice lunch all fixed up for you," Margaret said speaking for all three of the women.

"Actually, Margaret," I said, "I'm not real hungry right now. Fact is, I thought me and the boys would round up a fishing pole or two and head on down to old Parson's Creek outside of town. Why, who knows, we might even catch some fish ary there's still some left. It's been a long time, you know."

"Yes, Will," Margaret said in that knowing way of hers. "I suppose it has."

So me and Chance and Wash went fishing that afternoon. I don't rightly recall whether we caught any fish that day or not. What I do remember was that the war was over and my boys were back and we hadn't done anything but fight a bunch of Comancheros and damned Yankees and each other so far. Well, all of that was over now and things were getting back to normal, or as close to it as they should be.

Me, I was taking T. J. Faro's advice and catching up on some of those things I had always promised my boys I'd do with them.

Life was suddenly too short to do otherwise.

Printed in the United States
By Bookmasters